Cat Who Killed Lilian Jackson Braun

By the Same Author

The Cat Who Loved Harvey Weinstein
The Cat Who Sued Harvey Weinstein
The Cat Who Settled with Harvey Weinstein Out of Court
Harvey Weinstein's Cat: Omnibus Edition
The Cat Who Mistook His Wife for a Litterbox
The Cat Who Left a Surprise in the Cashmere Sweater Drawer
The Cat Who Tasted Like Chicken
Da Cat Who Chilled Wit Tupac
The Cat Who Was Convinced Herman Melville Wrote
  "Gold Diggers of 1935"
The Cat Who Fell to Earth and Then Was Flattened by a Steamroller
The Cat Who Put His Parents to Sleep
For Your Consideration: The Cat Who Bought Sixteen
  Full-Page Ads in Variety
The Cat Who Couldn't Go into Heat After He Went on Anti-depressants
The Cat Whose AOL Went AWOL
The Cat Who Would Be Kitty Carlisle
The Cat Who Threw a 90 M.P.H. Hairball
The Cat Who Hated Donald Rumsfeld
The Cat Who Was Deported by Donald Rumsfeld
Donald Rumsfeld and Harvey Weinstein: Omnibus Edition

Audiobook: The Cat Who Had the World's Worst Speech Impediment

The Cat Who Killed Lilian Jackson Braun

A Parody

By ROBERT KAPLOW

PHOENIX BOOKS

ISBN: 1-59777-541-X
Library of Congress Cataloging-In-Publication Data Available

Book Design by: Kerry DeAngelis, KL Design

Printed in the United States of America

Phoenix Books and Audio Inc.
9465 Wilshire Boulevard, Suite 315
Beverly Hills, CA 90212

10 9 8 7 6 5 4 3 2 1

The Cat Who Killed Lilian Jackson Braun is a work of satirical fiction. Although the novel is set against a background of real people and places, those people and places have been completely reinvented in the spirit of burlesque and parody. —R. K.

to my brother Richard

"...She agrees, sorrowfully, and slowly goes, reluctantly, home to the husband. I lie down in the dark bedroom and masturbate violently."

—CLIFFORD ODETS, 1940 JOURNAL

CHAPTER ONE

RETURNING PLATINUM

Someone must have traduced James Q., for without having done anything wrong, he heard a pounding on the door of his house.

The veteran children's book writer with worldwide experience pulled a robe over his 6'2" fiftyish, heavy-set, graying-haired, mournful-eyed, and luxuriantly-mustached frame.

As he arose, he heard the floor creak under the weight of his exposition.

Still, he thought, if they haven't read the other books, I've got to go through all this again.

He slept on the ground floor of a converted barn which he had modified with the small fortune he had accrued from his series of successful children's books.

Still the knocking came.

He nearly tripped over his Siamese cats, Ying-Tong and Poon-Tang, who were up, hungry, and bristling with suspicion. Ying-Tong was the amiable little female with a penchant for listening to old recordings of the Goon Show. Poon-Tang, the male, uttered a piercing but ambiguous, "Yo!"

He could make out two male voices beyond the door.

"Mr. Qafka! Mr. James Qafka! Are you there?"

He opened the door to see the two men, nearly identical, in close-fitting black suits.

"You've been traduced."

"Traduced?"

"Yes, sir. Traduced."

"Name?" asked one of the men.

"James MacIntosh Qafka."

"Sir, you've been traduced."

"Look," said Q., holding up a hand. "I've got to tell you, I'm not really a hundred-percent sure what 'traduced' means."

"Traduced?"

"Yes."

The men looked at each other.

They looked at the piece of paper they held.

One whispered something to the other.

"We'll be right back."

"Yes, we'll be back."

They quickly headed to the unmarked car which stood parked in the driveway. One of them muttered, "I *told* you to fucking look it up..."

A copy of *The New York Times* and *The Daily News* lay in the blue and yellow plastic bags in the driveway.

Q. brought the papers in the house as the phone was ringing. He ignored the phone, letting the answering machine kick in—though its volume was too low to monitor.

The *Times* headline read: *Admitting He Fought in Taliban, American Agrees to 20-Year Term.*

The Daily News headline read: *Johnny Jihad Cops a Plea.*

On the bottom of page one of the *Times* was a picture of a kindly-looking, white-haired woman, wearing oversized glasses; her chin on her fist, a sly smile on her lips. The caption read: *Popular Mystery Novelist Lilian Jackson Braun Dies Under Mysterious Circumstances.*

Q. looked for the same story in the *News*. Instead, there was only: *White Glove, White Hood: Michael Jackson to Dance at White Supremacy Rally.*

Ying-Tong and Poon-Tang were yowling again.

He prepared for them two bowls of Goan shrimp curry with steamed basmati rice. The shrimp had been stewed in ground coconut, red chile, ginger, garlic, and a little turmeric. Then he meticulously added fried eggs, sunny-side up, and two pieces of French bread. He placed the two steaming bowls down on the floor of his converted barn—careful to make sure Ying-Tong's green Chinese ceramic bowl went on the left side, and Poon-Tang's carved wooden bowl of Congolese teak went on the right.

"Enjoy yourself!" said Q.

The cats took one sniff and slinked away, irritated at not getting the dried-up stars of DeliCat they so loved.

Q., in the meantime, settled down to his customary green tea and stale glazed doughnut, as he continued to read the obituary:

<u>*Beloved Writer Found Decapitated in Gay Bar*</u>
It might have been a scene from one of her own mystery stories.

Beloved author of over 24 Cat Who... novels, Lilian

Jackson Braun's decapitated body was discovered some-time after two this morning in a toilet stall in a Greenwich Village bar.

The appearance of headless body was reported by club owner Thomas "Tom" Katz who was investigating why the restroom door had been locked for over two hours.

Mr. Katz at first thought Ms. Braun was throwing up in the toilet bowl, as the body was on its knees with its head in the toilet.

"I shook her shoulder; I said, 'Hey, fella, you all right? Then her body fell over, and I saw it had no head. I looked in the bowl. Under the sink. I couldn't find it," said Katz.

The body was identified by patrons who had seen the elderly writer earlier at the bar with a younger male com-panion.

Ms. Braun, who had been hospitalized earlier this year for what Dr. Alan Greenspan referred to as "infectious greed" was apparently recuperating rapidly and had been seen earlier that evening in tow with about a dozen male fans as they moved from bar to bar in the late-night world inhabited largely by the city's gay male population.

It seemed an incongruous setting to find the body of the delicate authoress, known to her millions of fans worldwide for the genteel, Norman Rockwell-like world of her novels: a world populated by charming eccentrics with names such as Derek Cuttlebrink, Osmond Hasselrich, Lena Inchpot, and Homer Tibbitt—and a menagerie of cats called Punky, Bootsie, Snuffles, and Shoo-Shoo. Ms. Braun's editor at G. P. Putnam's told the Times *he was shocked that her body had been discovered in such a location, and Ms. Braun's second husband Earl Bettinger told reporters early this morning that he was "astounded" at the location of his wife's body, adding that, "She lived the quiet life she portrayed in her novels: caring for her cats, preparing gourmet meals, working on her novels, and often going to bed by 8:30."*

Eyewitnesses, however, described a different woman altogether: a figure dressed in silver and black, surrounded by a boisterous pack of male devotees, cruising the West Village through a series of leather bars and dance clubs—a world of loud music and easy access to drugs. Police have traced her final night's journey through a series of clubs: The Azure Spheres, The Wiener in the Shrub, The Smiling Altar Boy, The Stork's Club, El Lumpumpadero, The Pastoral Pipe-Cleaner, and finally The Bulgin' Marbles, on Barrow Street, where her body was discovered.

Ms. Braun began writing professionally when she was sixteen, penning for the Detroit Times *a series of daily poems: "Or spoems I called them—they were sports poems."*

Q. found himself strangely moved by the obituary.

He had actually known Lilian Jackson Braun. They'd met at various book fairs, writers' roundtables, the Edgars, Diamond Dagger Award dinners. He'd been in attendance as a semi-celebrated children's book author. His *Little Blivet* series (*Little Blivet at the Zoo*; *Little Blivet Goes to Town*) had been great successes in their time, and now that the generation who had grown up with them had children of their own, the books were rarely out of print. Q. had tried to update the series in the late 1990s with more politically diversified and multi-cultural titles: *Little Blivet Has Three Daddies*, *Little Blivet Goes to Harlem*, *Little Blivet Meets Tito Puente*—but these were largely ignored by the critics and readers alike, going (as Q. liked to quip) directly from the printer to the remainder tables. "Returning platinum" was the phrase he used to describe the second half of his career. But still the royalty statements came in quarterly on *Little Blivet at the Zoo* and *Little Blivet Goes to Town*, and they more than supported him.

Readers adored the old titles; they desperately wanted him to be the friendly old writer who appeared in the books, Mr. Flapjacks—and so he often dressed the part: a white Panama hat, long white coat, lavender scarf around his neck, and a walking stick. Sometimes he caught himself in the mirror and couldn't believe his own absurdity. At an NCTE conference in Pittsburgh he was walking towards the convention center with Lilian Jackson Braun when they caught sight of themselves in the smoky glass of the corridor.

She said: "You look like a cross between Colonel Sanders and the Naked Civil Servant."

He'd said nothing. He smiled; twirled his cane merrily, tilted his hat, and sang "Mas Que Nada." She would later use the incident in her novel *The Cat Who Loved Sergio Mendez and Brazil '66*.

The phone was ringing again, and this time he turned up the volume.

"Mr. Qafka, this is Detective Ampersand from the Westfield Police Department. As you may know, the writer Lilian Jackson Braun was murdered last night, and her cell phone records indicate that the last call she made was to you—at 11:09 p.m. Can you give me a call and—"

He looked at the answering machine. There were three calls in its memory including this one.

He pressed the play/stop button.

"You have three messages," said the machine in its digitally-synthesized female voice.

Message one: "Saturday. Eleven-oh-two-p.m. Forty seconds." And then, unmistakably, the voice of Lilian Jackson Braun—its flat Michigan consonants. "Braun here." Her voice was close and a little breathless. "See what you can find out for me about the phrase 'lavender ink.' And don't mention this to anyone." Now he heard a jazz combo playing "Time After Time." "One minute," she said to someone in the background. And she hung up.

End of message, said the robot voice.

The other two messages were both from the cops.

He played Lilian's message again. "...the phrase 'lavender ink.'"

Braun had frequently called him up in the past to do light research. He, at least, was borderline computer-literate, and she was insufferably lazy about leaving the house.

A noise from the table, and Q. turned to see Ying-Tong scrabbling through *The Daily News*. It was as if she were trying to communicate something to him. She yowled, got up on her haunches, and urinated on the paper.

"Bad girl!" he shouted. He moved to pick up the soaked newspaper when he noticed the urine seemed to form an almost perfect circle around one particular story. It would not be the first time some seemingly preternatural power in the Siamese had given Q. a vital clue to a mystery.

The story, its inky newsprint smell mixing with the odoriferous cat urine, was headlined: *Britney Spears Gets Breasts Stuck in Cement Outside Graumann's Chinese Theatre.* And there was a photo of poor Britney, bent low over the sidewalk, wincing in pain—towel over her back, emergency medical team chipping away.

How was this connected with the mystery of Lilian Jackson Braun's death? he wondered.

Q. studied the photograph for a while longer, staring at the towel around Britney's shoulders. Then he moved to the bedroom and masturbated violently.

CHAPTER TWO

DIGNITY

Q. called the Westfield police station, but Detective Kingsley Ampersand along with detectives from the N.Y.P.D. were already at the Braun house on Hillside Avenue.

Even if Q. hadn't known where she lived, it wouldn't have been hard to find. Cars crawled by, the traffic backing down Lawrence. There was a light rain falling, as it must in all stories like these. Q. had walked anyway—enjoying the chill in the air. As he looked at the large estates and the wide streets that defined this part of Westfield, it struck him that Braun had mined the town for all its Currier-and-Ives charm. She had called her town Pickax, located "500 miles north of somewhere" in some nameless state that felt like Maine or Minnesota. It didn't matter where the stories took place, Q. thought; they were still insipid, obvious, infuriatingly slow, unbearably cute, and, of course, wildly successful. It must be the same audience who watched *Murder, She Wrote*, he thought: aging Angela Lansbury types who talked incessantly about their grandchildren. And meanwhile their grandchildren were in their bedrooms downloading pornography.

At any rate, the world described by Lilian Jackson Braun seemed to bear no connection at all with the world as Q. saw it.

"Mr. Qafka! Hi!"

From out of the rainy fog of his self-absorption stepped Gwen Duveen. Her perfume hit him first—with the kind of eye-watering intensity that only an eighteen year old could get away with—but, of course, she *was* eighteen or thereabouts. She had been a student in Q.'s Creative Writing class which he'd taught in the mornings last spring at Westfield High School. He didn't really need the money anymore (Little Blivet had taken care of that), but he enjoyed the complicated interplay of a classroom: the glint-eyed furies and the sudden explosions of joy that seemed to characterize adolescence. And there were moments of great stillness and sweetness in a classroom, when the room felt like a cathedral, and art represented the closest humans might come to perfection.

Gwen had graduated last spring; she stood before him now, slightly embarrassed as former students typically were, but genuinely happy to see him. There was, perhaps, an additional element to her embarrassment. Her father, Harold, was Q.'s former lawyer, and Q. had spent at least two formal evenings at the Duveen home: Harold's young blonde trophy-wife serving the peas in an eight-ton porcelain tray—the children: Gwen and Jesse, as awkward as he was, fumbling with the absurdly heavy silverware—everyone straining to be smart and memorable.

Gwen stood before him wearing a dusky white sleeveless shirt, horizontally striped with dark blue—like a French sailor—and below it white capris and sandals; her left index toe wore a silver ring. As a writer, Q. had trained himself to notice such things, and now it was like a machine that couldn't be stopped. He remembered from her journal that the toe-ring had been a gift from her boyfriend Brad—a guy who looked as if he'd been carved from wood—and then heavily lacquered.

"So how's your summer been?" she asked.

"Oh, fine. Been writing."

"Really? Watcha working on?"

"Another children's book."

"I can't believe you wrote *Little Blivet Goes to Town*. I mean, I grew up on that book. Everybody I know did."

Q. tried not to look at her chest as it strained its capacious load against the striped French shirt. The shirt was cut low enough that her great gifts were largely visible, as well as one pale blue shoulder strap.

OK, he said to himself, this is the style. That's all it is. She's not being provocative or alluring. And she finds your luxuriant fifty-year-old ass about as sexually exciting as a pair of dentures.

Her brown hair was short, almost bobbed. Moon-faced. Pale pink lipstick. Eyes like dark jade.

"—I mean, I couldn't believe when I signed up for Creative Writing that you would actually be the guy who wrote the *Little Blivet* books. I mean, that somebody actually even *wrote* them is pretty amazing to me. They're one of those things that seem like they've always been there. You know? Like *The Wizard of Oz* or something. I mean, I can't imagine someone actually writing *The Wizard of Oz*—"

He could have told her how he'd met Harold Arlen, who wrote the music to *The Wizard of Oz* film, but he was thinking about Brad having unlimited access to those breasts. He imagined (things getting a little blurry now) Brad unbuttoning her white capris; the pale blue Victoria's Secret underwear matching her poor straining brassiere.

"—I'm taking cooking lessons this summer," she said, her voice going up as if this were a question. "It's kinda silly, but I'm enjoying it. We're doing pastries all week—"

Oh, God, Gwen, he heard Brad's voice in his head. *Oh, damn*— as lacquered Brad spurted into her face a load so dense and voluminous that her nostrils were immediately sealed shut.

"—we're doing raspberry tarts today. I'm actually kind of excited. And I'm late, too..."

"I'll be on my way then."

He touched his walking stick to his Panama hat, and he strolled on towards Hillside, the lovable, eccentric, and amiably neutered children's book writer.

Oh, damn, said Brad, still spewing like some kind of insane adolescent fire extinguisher. *Damn, damn!*

Lilian Jackson Braun had chosen to live on Hillside Avenue, at the same address where John List had slaughtered his entire family in 1971. For Braun it had been a sort of grim joke, and it would later inspire her novella: *The Cat Who Killed His Entire Family Including His Mother and Then Casually Walked Out the Door and Disappeared for Eighteen Years, Remarried, and Was Discovered Living In Virginia Under an Assumed Name.* Putnam shortened the name to *The Cat Who Made a Booboo*, and the novel was short-listed for the Booker Prize but lost to Michael Chabon's *Life is a Big But: The Oprah Winfrey Story.*

A news helicopter circled overhead, and the curbside was filled with satellite trucks—their long, spiked masts raised like terrible, privacy-eating insects. Bright banks of lights held aloft on scaffolding burned through the mist, and Q. wondered what anyone hoped to see. The poor woman had died in lower Manhattan, not here. Here she had only sat in her second-floor study—with her blue IBM Selectric typewriter—staring out the window at the pear tree, writing her shitty mysteries. OK, he thought, "shitty" was too strong a word. Her tidy mysteries. That was a good word for the obituaries. The author of tidy little mysteries. Of course, in the universe of Lilian Jackson Braun, the concept of shit didn't quite exist. It wasn't in keeping with the immaculate tastefulness of the stories— but, Q. thought, it might make a good opening scene. Her next novel starts with old James Quilleran sitting on the throne, closing his eyes in agony—he's sweating—and, finally, three weeks' worth of psillium husks gathers its collective force and out slides this enormous, bloated, toilet-stuffing, rank-brown zucchini. It clogs the toilet; it clogs the neighbor's toilet; the entire city's sewer system is backing up. The cats are screeching, standing on the bookcases as the water cascades over the bowl. Quilleran is standing there with his pants down, plunging away. The water's turning the color of mahogany.

Good opening, thought Q., as he walked up onto the lawn on Hillside.

Up on the hill of the front lawn, amid the reporters and the investigators, stood Detective Kingsley Ampersand: large-stomached, slightly goofy-looking, head shaped like a pencil eraser.

"So she called you," said Ampersand.

"You going to light that thing?" asked Q. He nodded towards the slim cigar jammed in Ampersand's mouth.

"You were the last person she called." He took out a notebook—entered the date. "How the hell do you spell your last name again?"

"I could hear jazz music in the background."

"You remember that?"

"It's on my answering machine tape."

"You still have the tape?"

"I might. She asked me to research the phrase 'lavender ink.'"

"What the fuck is that?"

Q. shrugged.

"Is it 'ink' like you write with or 'inc.' like the company?"

"Can't help you, detective."

"This whole thing pisses me off," he said. He sucked on the unlit cigar, held the imaginary smoke in his lungs, and then violently coughed it out. He scribbled down 'lavender ink.'"

"What pisses you off?"

"I stand here," he said. "Getting my shoes muddy. I write down the goddamn clues in the evidence book. I work with the crime lab. I dust the house for fingerprints. I get the call at 3:15 in the fucking morning, and you know what happens?" He touched the top of his head. "Look at this, will you?" He parted the already thin hair and rooted around until he found a tiny pink growth on his skull, about the size of a thumbtack. "Does this look all right to you?"

"What?"

"This thing. I got a thing here on my head."

"I don't see it."

"Look. Look where my finger is."

"Yeah?"

"You see it?"

"I see something."

"What is it? Does it look all right?"

"I'm not a doctor."

"No, but does it look bad?"

"No, it's pink. It looks like a fatty cyst."

"A fatty cyst, right? That's all. It's not cancer, right?"

"It's pink; it looks like nothing."

"'Cause I got bit by a tick on my head and now I feel like there's something on my head all the time, like spiders or something."

"Go see a doctor."

"I saw three of them. What the fuck do they know?

But, basically, you think it looks all right?"

"Kingsley, I'm not a doctor."

"Right." He sucked on the unlit cigar. "You're the amateur detective, I forgot. See that's what pisses me off. I do the work; I mean, the real schlepping, the stupid work, the grunt work, the telephone work, all the dead-end interviews that everybody knows will lead to nothing. And what do you do? You solve the case."

"Hardly."

"Of course it's you. I've read this series before. You're the star. I'm a fucking walk-on. I'm fucking Inspector Lestrade. I'm the dufus with the wrong theory. Wouldn't it be great, just once, if *I* solved the crime, and *you* didn't? Wouldn't that make a great surprise ending?"

"It's a real possibility."

"No, it isn't. Not unless I get my own series. And that's never going to happen."

"Why not? Like *Laverne and Shirley*?"

"No. They never promote from within. Two more years and I'm out anyway."

"You're retiring?"

"Yup. No more Westfield Police Department. You know what a buddy of mine said who left the department this year?"

"What?"

"He said: 'The minute I get out of this place, the first thing I'm doing is going down to the nearest bus station and suck cock until I get my dignity back.'"

CHAPTER THREE

PRIZE WINNER

Q.'s head was filled with questions, and in order to keep the plot straight, he repeated them to himself: How had America's most beloved authoress—modest, cautious, civilized—come to die in a dark, disreputable bar in lower Manhattan—her body mutilated? What had dear Ying-Tong been trying to indicate when she drew his attention to the Britney Spears'-breasts-stuck-in-cement story? And what was the meaning of Braun's final phone call? The cryptic reference to "lavender ink"?

He parked his car at White Rose in Highland Park—a hamburger joint run by ex-cons where he was meeting Philip Roth for lunch. He knew Roth fairly well. Roth was teaching a summer session at Rutgers—a sort of answer to Ralph Wiley's *Why Black People Tend to Shout* which Roth was calling: *Why Jews Tend to Be Cheap*. The university, of course, wouldn't print that title in their catalogue and so Roth resubmitted it as: *Ethnic Stereotypes and Why They are Accurate*.

The glass windows were fogged; the air smelled like a thousand cheeseburgers and those cheap dill slices that come from a can. Roth and Q. had met here nearly every Friday all summer, and Q. looked forward to hearing his take on the death of Lilian Jackson Braun.

Roth was sitting at the white Formica counter by the front window, ceramic cup of coffee in his hand, *The New York Post* propped against the glass. The *Post* was running the Lilian Jackson Braun story on page one. *Killer Gets Head in Village Bathroom* read the enormous headline.

As usual, Roth was playing Brenda Lee's "Rockin' Around the Christmas Tree" on the old jukebox. He was wearing the same green military jacket he'd been wearing for years—and he looked particularly grim and sallow.

"What the hell do you keep playing this for?" said Q. "It's goddamn August."

"This is a great record. A great melody. Listen to the middle part." He held up a hand like a conductor, and he sang along with: "'You will get a sentimental feeling'... There's *melody* there. This isn't just a rock 'n' roll record."

"Yes, it's a high-water mark in American popular song."

Roth looked up, his eyes suddenly burning with the passion of an actor who's got an audience. You saw in his face the little Jewish boy relentlessly determined to prove he's the smartest one in the class—and everybody else just wants to beat his ass. "Did I tell you I met the guy who wrote that song? Johnny Marks? The same guy who wrote 'Rudolph the Red-Nosed Reindeer'?"

"Another masterpiece," Q. said. "A talent right up there with Cole Porter and Rodgers and Hammerstein."

Roth snorted. "Rodgers and Hammerstein! Two Jews from New York who wrote the most goyish music in theatrical history." He sang: "'My boy Velvel; he'll be tall and as tough as—' you see, you can't rhyme 'Velvel.' Rodgers and Hammerstein spent their whole careers hiding from the fact that they were Jewish. Look at them: *Carousel*, *Oklahoma!*, Mary Martin! Oy! Disneyland! No wonder America ate them up."

"What did you want them to write about?" said Q. "'Oh, What a Beautiful Shtetel'? You can't rhyme 'shtetel' either."

"You rhyme it with apostrophe L-L," snapped back Roth—still the smartest kid in the class. "Even this old luncheonette'll..."

Some tall businessman was jostling towards the counter, asking for a large glass of ice water.

"But I did meet Johnny Marks."

"Did you order yet?"

"You're not letting me finish. I met him at the NPR downlink on 42nd Street; I was waiting to do an interview when this old guy comes shuffling in with a long black coat with a big egg stain on the lapel, and he gives his name to the engineer"—Roth lowered his voice to growl—'Johnny Marks.' And I said, 'Are you the Johnny Marks who wrote 'Rudolf the Red-Nosed Reindeer'? And he says, 'Yeah. Who the hell are you?'" Roth laughed at the memory. "And then he hit on me! The old, disgusting son-of-a-bitch hit on me!" He lowered his voice again. "'Say, young fella, are you doing anything this afternoon?' Christ, I sound like Arte Johnson on *Laugh-In*. 'How about a walnetto?' I watch *Laugh-In* every night now. It's on some drecky cable station. I watch it instead of writing.

It's like this terribly embarrassing archive from a lost period of time. 1968. It's nearly completely laughless now—and I'm *riveted*. Absolutely mesmerized. That somebody actually once looked into a television camera and said, 'Sock it to me, sock it to me, sock it to me.'"

A shower of water and ice fell from above—right on top of Roth's head, as the tall businessman accidentally spilled his order all over the place.

They mopped each other up with paper towels as Q. revealed that he had been the last person Lilian Jackson Braun had telephoned on the night of her death.

"What the hell did she phone *you* for?" said Roth. He was still wiping ketchup and onions from what little hair he had left. "Was she looking for a kindred spirit of mediocrity?"

"That's below the belt," Q. said.

"Her characters don't exist below the belt. Sexless grandmas in Cutesytown collecting limited-edition dinner plates and fussing with the kitty-cats."

"Have you ever even read one of her novels?"

"Claire used to read that dreck. They were all over the house. I couldn't get past page six."

Q. was carrying two of the novels, and he spread them before Roth. "They're fairly innocuous."

Roth grabbed *The Cat Who Went Underground* and flipped it open about a quarter way through. His eyes narrowed behind his reading glasses. He shook his head. "Look at this." He read: *"He was one of five thousand big, healthy, young blond fellows in Moose County."* He looked around to an imaginary audience. "Can you believe this? Five thousand big, healthy, young *blond* fellows? Why doesn't she call the book: *The Cat Who Was Only Following Orders*? Big, healthy, young blond fellows. Yeah, right. Paging Martin Bormann. These are sick fantasies, James. A goyish wet-dream in which the whole world is Bar Harbor and everybody wears button-down shirts and drinks martinis. Jesus Christ, they should put a sticker on the cover. Winner of Anti-Zionist Prize. Five thousand big, healthy, young blond fellows. Christ, it's Garrison Keillorland. Let's celebrate America. Just make sure no Jews with their big, hairy erections get in the picture, all right? And the blacks? Hey, they don't even leave footprints in books like this. So who picks up the garbage in Mooseville?" His voice suddenly got Old Southern. "Why it's ole Zekeland McCornhole, heheheheh. Ole Zekeland's been running around this here refuse dump for thirty odd years now, heheheh, he's a rough and ready old geezer— why ole Zekeland might be a little unshaved, you know, and might not be the most *grammatical* feller you ever met, but, by jimminy, when you need a tree taken away or you can't get your old pick-up started—why old Zeke'll be there by the time you can say 'kosher le pesach.' That is, unless he's sitting home jerking off to *Teenage Rump Reamers, Volume Seven*."

"I think you made your point."

But Roth's eyes were blazing now—and his voice had risen in volume to the point where strangers in White Rose were looking at him.

He grabbed another book: *The Cat Who Went Up the Creek*. With ostentatious randomness, he stuck a finger in the book and read: "*Both young people were vibrantly attractive. She had a tumble of dark hair and merry eyes; he looked wholesomely healthy like a camp counselor.* I can't believe this!" cried Roth. "Another one! 'Wholesomely healthy! LIke a *camp* counselor.' *Camp*. Do you get it? Round up old Heshie Heshkowitz with his beak and his books and the little mole on his cheek and send him off to camp. I think these books should be burned."

"You're insane."

"Insane, huh? Winner of the National Book Critics Circle Award for *Patrimony*. The Pen/Faulkner Award for *Operation Shylock*. National Book Award for *Sabbath's Theatre*. Pulitzer Prize for *American Pastoral*. And the Ambassador Book Award of the English Speaking Union for *I Married a Communist*."

"*I Married a Shiksa* is more like it."

"And all of them in the 1990's!"

"Achh!" Q. dismissed them all. "They had *rachmonis* for you, that's all. The old Jew won't shut up. Give him something for Christ's sake—so we don't look like anti-Semite bastards."

"I got the National Medal of Arts Award from the White House!"

"From Clinton, for Christ's sake. That doesn't count. He pulled his dick out of Monica's face for five seconds—cleared his head—and said, 'OK, we'll give it to the Jew... Now, back to work, bitch!'"

"You're jealous, that's all."

"Philip, you're a great writer. But I couldn't finish *The Human Stain*. I'm supposed to believe that character is black! Come on! And *The Dying Animal*? It reads like a dirty old man: 'her tits, her tits, her magnificent tits, her glorious tits.'"

"That was a set-up, for Christ's sake."

"Her luminous tits. Her radioactive tits."

"She gets breast cancer at the end. That was a set-up."

"It was dirty old man stuff; it's, I don't know, just *unbecoming*."

"Old men can't think about sex? That's all they *do* think about for Christ's sake. I'm being honest."

"Then it's unbecomingly honest," said Q. "It's like those Woody Allen movies where he's got himself playing the romantic lead to some twenty-year-old girl—and his bald spot is glinting under the klieg lights and he's looking like her grandfather."

"And you know what the alternative to *unbecoming* is? It's bullshit like this." He threw *The Cat Who Went Up the Creek* to the floor. "I'm telling the truth." He coughed a little on his double-cheese-with-onions. "You can't handle the truth." He coughed again—this time more violently than before. He spat phlegm into his napkin. "You never see *this* in one of her novels. Some old Jew taking a good *chrock* into a napkin."

"Are you all right?"

"You know what this means, don't you? It means I die later in the book."

Q. laughed.

He smiled sourly as if to say: You'll see.

"Sorry if I was little rough there," Q. said.

He waved a dismissive hand. "That's what Jews do. They scream at each other in fury, jealousy, and self-punishing cynicism. *Uh-main*. Look, Q. you're the master author of such deathless works as *Little Blivet Gets a Circumcision*."

"Good title."

"The book comes with a little piece of velcro foreskin so the kid can act it out. Like Pat the Bunny for Hymietown. Listen. I'm all for honesty. Look at poor Jonathan Franzen. He said what every single writer in America felt: that Oprah is an idiot and what right did a fucking talk show host have to define the literary tastes of America? He just *said* it."

"And for his integrity he got his testicles handed to him on a plate."

"A *milchadick* plate, too. But you have to respect him for standing up to her. Who else would? She was like Walter Winchell. If she mentioned your book you were a millionaire; if she froze you out, your career was over." He shook his head in disbelief. "Oprah was deciding America's literary taste! Next we're going to have P. Diddy writing *The New York Times* theatre reviews. "Yo, not since the Golden Age of American Popular Music has the Broadway stage been graced with a musical like 'Planet Booty'. The audience was lifted aloft on songs like 'Oh, What a Beautiful Booty,' 'The Booty with the Fringe on

Top,' and 'I'm Gonna Wash That Man Right Out of My Booty.'"

Roth coughed badly again—then raised a warning finger to me. "They're setting this up in act one. Keep your eyes open."

"Nobody's dying, Philip. This is a parody book. You know, like Sol Weinstein's Oy-Oy Seven series. Like *Loxfinger*. Don't worry, you'll hate it. You don't think anything's funny."

"Not true." He sipped his coffee. "I reread *Portnoy* the other day. Now that book is fucking funny."

CHAPTER FOUR

AEROBICS

Ying-Tong and Poon-Tang were keeping an aloof distance, apparently punishing Q. for his absence.

The silvery female, Ying-Tong, stood silhouetted in the window of the office, and the play of warm, brilliant light in her luminous fur and on the green and white hardback copy of *Franny and Zooey* that lay next to her was in itself well worth beholding.

The black male, Poon-Tang, walked deftly along the exposed rafters.

Q. still had time before he was visited by the children's library group. He suddenly remembered the clipping of Britney's appearance at Graumann's Chinese Theatre that Ying-Tong had drawn to his attention.

What possible relevance could it have to the death of Lilian Jackson Braun?

He entered "Britney photos" into his desktop computer's search-engine, but it yielded nothing more than the usual collection of press releases and digitally-altered pornography. He wondered what Britney's mother must think of these images of her naked daughter sitting on a kitchen counter-top jamming a full-sized yellow squash between her legs. He thought it might make a good poster for the Vegan Movement.

By now he was completely distracted from his original research—and he clicked on a link called "Britney blowjob photos".

The screen bloomed in half a dozen pop-up windows. "XXX Celebrities: Britney Bare Nipple Video."

The doorbell rang.

He could see, outside the small door-framing window, a group of about twelve boys and girls from the Children's Summer Reading Circle—with Mrs. Marjorie Hudak, looking like Virginia Woolf in a flowered sundress, staring at the door.

He guiltily clicked the close window on his screen—and another pop-up opened: "Britney Sucking Two Dicks." He clicked on close again.

Another pop-up: "101 Naked Cheerleader Thumbnails."

"Come on," he said.

He was clicking on everything now. Close. Close.

Mrs. Hudak was knocking on the window. "James? James, are you there?"

"One second!" he called.

The screen was filled with a huge animated advertisement for *SororityStrap-ons.com*.

And now the mouse froze; the image froze—filling the screen: *SororityStrap-ons.com*—two skanky thirty-year-old women pretending they were teenagers, adjusting the black leather straps of some monstrous sexual appliance.

"James!" came Mrs. Hudak's voice. "Did you forget you had an appointment?"

"One minute!"

He couldn't get the machine to shut down. All the controls were frozen. Even the emergency shutdown was frozen.

He finally moved to unplug the damn thing, but there were eight plugs jammed into a surge protector: all the cables hopelessly snarled.

"James?"

She was inside the house. He'd left the door unlocked.

"James, are you all right?"

"Yes, yes, Marjorie, just finishing some research."

"Well, maybe we can watch you. Children, come on inside."

He pulled the three-prong plug out from the back of the computer, and, in a crackle of static, the screen went mercifully dark.

"Have we caught you at a bad time, James?"

"No, not at all. I always have time for my readers. Here, let me put on my costume. We might as well give them the whole show."

The children sat on the floor around his chair as he put on his obligatory Panama hat, lavender cravat, and long white coat.

"He's Mr. Flapjacks!" said one child.

"I'm always glad to allow my readers into my home," Q. said, and he settled a little messily into a green wicker chair. Under the full load of his girth, the poor chair immediately broke a leg.

The children laughed.

"You're fat," said a little girl in a pale blue dress.

"Laura," cautioned Mrs. Hudak.

"Now, boys and girls, you all read Mr. Qafka's wonderful *Little Blivet Goes to Town*, and I'm sure you all have questions you'd like to ask him. How does an author work? Where does he get his ideas from? What other books has Mr. Qafka written? What's he working on now? We all saw him working so hard on his computer when we came in. Let's start with any questions you have for Mr. Q. OK? Who's got the first question? Raise your hands now."

The kids sat looking at each other. At the floor. Two boys hit each other.

"Doesn't anybody have a question for Mr. Qafka?"

Finally, the girl in the pale blue dress raised her hand.

"Yes, Laura, what's your question?"

"Can I go to the bathroom?"

When Q. had signed a dozen books, and his youthful fans had left, he returned to the Britney newspaper clipping that Ying-Tong had so conspicuously indicated. He turned it over. There was half a theatre review for the McCarter Theatre revival of *June Moon*.

The cat was obviously pointing him in some direction.

He stared again at Britney kneeling before the cement of Graumann's—wincing in pain. *Britney Bare Nipple Video.*

Please.

He got up and drank another cup of green tea.

Britney Sucking Two Dicks.

No. No.

He looked at the framed photograph of Polly Thompson

that he kept on his upright piano. She was the love of his life—and, strangely, was never at home during this or any other novel in the series.

His editor, Joanna at HarperCollins, had suggested recently that he work on another Little Blivet story. "Write it Old School," she'd said. "Very tame. Charming. And funny." She had even suggested a title: *Little Blivet Keeps a Diary*. He kept reassuring her that he was working on it, but it felt increasingly hopeless.

What kind of animal is Little Blivet?

This was the question he had been expecting from the library kids—but, of course, such a question presupposed that someone had actually *opened* the book and read a few sentences—an assumption that eliminated most of his current readers. He had no real answer for the question anyway. Born of two solidly human parents, Little Blivet resembled something between a squirrel and a ferret. He spoke English but found few friends among the humans.

Q. thought, rather dismally, that he wrote so convincingly about Little Blivet because Q. himself still felt like a small animal—a hopeless misfit—dazzled and delighted and saddened by the world—capable of being moved to tears by the complexity of an automobile interior, the folds in a pair of black trousers, the window light caught in the rim of a teacup—but unable to share the urgency of that vision with anyone.

He raised his eyes to a card he'd tacked to the corkboard. "Dear Mr. Q.: Thanks for the lovely Creative

Writing class. You managed to keep us all a little on edge, and that inspired us all to be a little braver than we otherwise might have been..." Alongside the card was a colored photograph of the eleven students who had taken the course. They were standing in front of a summery-lush tree on the high school lawn. Nicole, Avery, Gwen—what Westfield names they had—bled from the bark of ancient Protestant oaks. There was Gwen Duveen—in that damn low-necked sailor's shirt again, the thin spaghetti strap of a blue brassiere tantalizingly caught on the joint of a creamy shoulder—

No. No more.

He would find resolve.

Q. got up to wash his hands before heading over to Braun's place. He'd told Bettinger, her husband, that he'd investigate the case privately—parallel to the official investigation. Bettinger had seemed relatively indifferent to the death of his wife. And maybe that, itself, was a clue.

He squirted the liquid soap in his hands.

It dripped messily through his fingers.

Gwen Duveen.

He looked at himself in the mirror.

Resolve. That's all it takes. Iron resolve.

Then he masturbated violently and washed up.

"I feel *much* more relaxed," he assured himself. He liked to think of it as a kind of low-level aerobic workout.

OK, *extremely* low-level.

CHAPTER FIVE

SOMETHING FROM THE 1930's

In the universe of the Lilian Jackson Braun books, charmingly eccentric characters often found themselves in the Dimsdale Diner—nicknamed the Dismal Diner—home of "bad food and worse coffee," located at the intersection of Pickax Road and Ittibittiwasee Road.

But this morning, Q. found himself on plain old East Broad Street, sitting in Vicki's Diner eating a rather delicious BLT on whole-wheat toast. He frequented the diner because his high school girlfriend had been named Vicki, and he always half-hoped that she might have returned to town and opened the restaurant. Vicki, however, never seemed to actually be in the place. Like Duffy in "Duffy's Tavern" or his girlfriend Polly Thompson (now doing research in Italy), Vicki was more talked about than seen.

A sign hung in the window:

amous

or

ine

oods

The large "F" had fallen off some months earlier.

"You're eatin' poison, you know," said a voice behind him.

Stumpy Rabinowitz joined him at the counter. Stumpy

was a charmingly eccentric Vietnam veteran. He was missing an arm and a few teeth. His stomach bulged through his thin white tee-shirt, and he carried with him a massive cloud of body odor—a stench that penetrated everything in his orbit. You fell in the shadow of his fetid fog and you felt your immune system being instantly compromised. Sparse red hair and a splotchy red beard completed his portrait. "You gotta be careful, man. What you eat. An artist like you."

"Hey, Stump."

"Bacon. Loaded with fat, salt, and nitrites. Plus the meat itself is a biohazard. Didn't you read *Fast Food Nation*, man? *There's shit in the meat.*"

Q. had been poised to take another bite. "Thanks." He put the sandwich down.

"Processed white flour? Garbage. Turns to sugar in, like, five seconds. Type Two diabetes, man. You better wash it down with an insulin smoothie. Look at this. Pale green lettuce? Nutritionally inert, man. Got nothing in it except the illusion that you're eating vegetables. Pale, shitty, processed tomato—genetically engineered for a shelf life of six months? *Frankenfood*, man. Monsanto-burger. Farmers can't even replant the seeds, man, 'cause Monsanto has *copywritten* the seeds. Can you imagine that? They got a copyright on a tomato. You're eating dead food, man. Corporate food."

"And what the hell are you eating?"

He took a long slurp from his mug. "Black coffee, man." He smiled and the coffee dripped through the yellow, rotten teeth. "Hot and black. Just like my women!" Stumpy laughed evilly and choked down some more black coffee. "Caffeine, man. I eat it. It's alive! It's the *life force*. Vicki's got special beans for me behind the counter—organic shit from the mountains. You're eating pig corpses and techno-lettuce, but I'm eating life. Coffee beans, man. Each one a seed! Each one a DNA blueprint for a tree. All that life packed into a hard little seed—and I'm ingesting it!" He sang: "I got life, brother!" He laughed again, and the coffee dribbled down his chin. "I survived Agent Orange, man! If it doesn't kill you, it makes you stronger!"

Stumpy's gaze fell on *The Westfield Leader* which Q. was reading. On the cover was *Westfield's Most Beloved Resident Murdered*, and there was the same photograph of Lilian Jackson Braun that every other paper had run.

"Most beloved resident, huh!" said Stumpy. "Like shit."

"She probably was."

He turned to Q. with a new wave of foul body odor roiling off his overheated body. "She was a sicko, man. A dirty sicko, man. You pick up one of the cinderblocks in Hell, and she's what's crawling around underneath."

"What are you talking about?"

"She had a secret life, man."

"And how do you know?"

"I know *everything* in this fucking town, man. Stumpy stands in the shadows! Stumpy's out after midnight! Stumpy's looking through windows! Stumpy sees *every-*

thing!" He moved in closer—it was like somebody shoving his anus in your face. "Por ejemplo, Stumpy knows that a certain lady in this town is interested in a certain celebrated children's book author."

"You're crazy."

"I'm talking about sweet dee-sire, man. Animal desire! But deeply fucked up! It all comes down to the *ani-mahhl!"*

"*You* are fucked up, Stump." Q. got up. "I like you, man. I mean, I enjoy psychotics and all, but you are *really* fucked up. I think you need to eat some food. You can finish my sandwich."

"Death, man. Dead food!" He put his hands over the BLT like a demented healer. "No *field!* No life. It's as dead as Lily Jackson Braun."

Q. paid old Nat for his lunch. Nat was a holdover from when the place was the Towne Lunch. He'd been a vaudeville magician, and at the slightest prompting now he'd take out an old folded piece of stationery that read "The Astounding Rivoli"—and beneath it, in tiny printed script: "Please excuse brevity, note written in haste in dressing room."

Q. thought that someday he'd make a great minor character in a murder mystery. It was too bad this wasn't it.

The voices in Q.'s head were loud with questions—and they all spoke at once. He was driving towards Hillside Avenue to pay a condolence call on Earl Bettinger.

Did Stumpy have any idea what he was talking about? A secret life for Lilian Jackson Braun?

And what of the "lady" who was interested in a certain celebrated children's book writer?

But who could really listen to that scumbag—with his yellowed teeth and skin like petroleum jelly.

A car honked at Q.—a hand waved hello out a window—it was a blond-haired parent of one of his students—but she was gone before he could even come up with a name.

Q. wasn't hard to recognize on the road. He drove an ancient peanut butter-colored Checker Marathon.

The yellow caution tape has been removed from the Braun/Bettinger house, and the satellite trucks were gone, but the slow crawl of thrill-seekers still moved by. You could see fingers pointing through the opened car windows.

Bettinger was waiting for him in the kitchen. The house smelled of cooking: abundant odors of garlic and roast chicken and wine.

Classical music was playing.

"This recipe," explained Bettinger, whose college-professor demeanor contrasted absurdly with the cooking bib he was wearing: a large cartoon of a naked Betty Boop holding out a silver tray—her left breast resting plumply on the tray: *Take a bite?* said the caption, "was a favorite of Mademoiselle Fernande Garvin of the Bordeau Wine Information Bureau."

Q. stood there in quiet astonishment. He had expected to find grief: the shades pulled down, a few sympathy fruit baskets with their battered pears and tiny jam jars that no one would ever use. Instead, it looked and smelled like a dinner party.

He killed her, thought Q. Any police officer in the world would be convinced that he's celebrating. But if Bettinger really had done it, then why on earth would he be so conspicuous in his indifference?

"First the chicken quarters are *dredged* with flour—isn't that a wonderful word? And then browned. Then we replace the oil in the skillet with seasonal tomatoes. Stir in a little flour for a natural gravy. We simmer for about twenty minutes. Then we add a dry white Bordeaux, mushrooms, and, lastly, *finely-chopped* garlic."

He poured this mixture of wine and herbs from a yellow mixing bowl, and it crackled and hissed and scalded and steamed in the large iron skillet. He sniffed the air. "Ah! Wouldn't your little kitties enjoy this! Don't worry; I'll send some home with you." He covered the skillet. "And we simmer it for perhaps another twenty minutes."

He set the timer to twenty.

"Our appetizer will be zucchini *a la Greque*," he said, raising the lid on another pan. "Sautéed young zucchini from our garden with fresh tarragon, parsley, lemon, garlic, and *tabasco*. Sensational."

"I don't know what to say," said Q.

"Yes, I know," said Bettinger. "You expected to find me sitting in a dark house eating leftover Sloppy Joe's."

He took off his apron and washed his hands. He was

tall and thin with long, expressive fingers that resembled bamboo shoots—and a fussiness of manner which seemed to preclude any notion that he could be a killer.

"I think they actually suspected me at first," he said. He sat at the polished black kitchen table. "I understand that in ninety percent of the cases, it actually *is* the husband. They questioned me—sat me down in the interviewing room at the station, and I see there is a pair of handcuffs attached to the table. 'Are those for me?' I asked, half-seriously. 'Not yet,' said the cop. *Seriously* said that. 'Not yet.' I was speechless. They actually thought I might be capable of that." He put his fingertips on Q.'s hand. This was a habit that Q. had never liked; he was always touching him: the hand on the shoulder, the affectionate tousling of the hair. It was, he supposed, an attempt at intimacy—but it only made him feel uneasy— as if all the conversation was just a polite preamble to the evening's real purpose: cocksucking *a la Greque*.

"Anyway," Bettinger continued, "*one* of them was fairly civilized. At least today he was. They checked out my story."

"You had an alibi?"

"I was at the theatre. Unfortunately alone. But I was there. Could tell them all about the play. Here's the other ticket." He pointed to a ticket held under a magnet on the refrigerator door. "*June Moon*: the old George S. Kaufman chestnut. At the McCarter. Silly but enjoyable. Of course, Lilian and I were supposed to go together. Yes, *that's* likely. But she bought me the subscription for my birthday."

He touched Q.'s hand again. "You know, it's *all* theatre in this house. There was little love lost between us two." He rested his fingers on his chest. "For heaven's sake, I *told* the officers that. That this marriage was more or less a tired joke. An *elaborate* public relations exercise. Lilian Jackson Braun: elegant octogenarian—firmly rooted in family values—ex-American history professor hubby at her side as she climbs the dais to accept the Edgar Award." He shook his head. "If they really gave away awards in the name of Mr. Edgar Allan Poe, they should give them to twenty-eight-year-old men who married their thirteen-year-old cousins. Of course, that means they'd have to give them exclusively to Southern writers."

The timer rang, and they dined on a truly delicious meal.

He stood smoking French cigarettes on the front porch.

The sun was going down and a few fireflies still sparkled across the wide expanse of the lawn. Their lights were mirrored in the headlights which moved like a procession in front of the house. And there on the bottom of the driveway was a growing luminary of candles, flowers, tribute-wreaths.

"I used to have to smoke outside," he said. "No real reason to do it anymore, I guess. I can foul up any room I want. But here I stand." He flicked his lit cigarette out onto the lawn. "Look at that crap," he said, nodding towards the luminary. "Come pay homage to America's most beloved mystery writer... I'll have Aldo throw it all out tomorrow."

"You feel no sentimentality for her?"

"Habit. That's what I feel. Her voice. 'Earl, take out the garbage.' I guess it's terrible to say, but I don't feel anything particularly sad about her passing. The wake is Saturday. I suppose I'll stand there with some sort of blank expression on my face—something approximating grief—and shake hands and mumble words—and get through the day—and come home to this big empty house. Of course, it was empty most of the time she was here, too."

"She did *live* here?"

"She was rarely home. And I think her secretary Maxine wrote most of those piece-of-shit mysteries. God, did you ever try to read one? *Ghastly...* No, she was out most nights."

"At her age?"

"She was an insane son-of-a-bitch, may she rest in peace. A lascivious horror."

Q. looked astonished.

"It was her other identity," he said. "Her shadow." He put his hand on Q.'s shoulder. "Everybody's got a shadow, haven't they?"

Q. smiled and moved further down the porch railing. "Why have you stayed with her all these years?"

He looked out towards the street—and took another step closer to Q. "Where am I going? Because of her I'm a wealthy man. I have no motive to leave her *or* kill her. Other than my own physical revulsion at her presence.

You know they say as you grow older, as a man, your testosterone level begins falling off, and your estrogen level begins rising. You get in touch with your 'feminine side.' But, in my case, you know, I feel the estrogen levels must have been pretty high since... I can remember."

There was no place further to move down the porch, so Q. stood with his back to the railing—and one foot in front of him like a cow-catcher. It was entertaining to watch Bettinger bobbing and weaving—unable to get physically closer.

"Does the term 'lavender ink' mean anything to you? It was the last message I received from her. She asked me to look up the significance of the term."

"It does ring a sort of dim gong."

"That's all she said: to look up 'lavender ink.'"

"This sounds more and more like one her terrible mysteries, doesn't it? Someone dies muttering, 'Rosebud,' and it's not until two hundred and thirteen pages later we find out it's the nickname of Marion Davies' pudendum. Poor Marion. That's all she's remembered for these days: that William Randolph Hearst called her twat 'Rosebud.'" Bettinger chuckled. "The moral is that we better tread rather carefully around artists. They write the epitaphs we're remembered by. I suppose I should be careful around *you*. Who knows what you'll say about me in one of your stories. Will I be the Middlebury teacher of the year? The elegant heartbroken widower? The confidante of the narrator? Or perhaps, if I'm very lucky, the love interest?"

Q. thought: *Or the repressed homosexual?*

"No. Not me," Q. said. "I respect you too much to ever use you in a book. Besides, you're too complicated and contradictory to use in a book."

"Complicated and contradictory," Bettinger said. "I think that's almost a compliment, isn't it?"

"And what about 'lavender ink'? You said it means something?"

"Yes... something from the 1930's... but I'm not thinking that clearly. Maybe you can come back tomorrow?"

When the house is empty and the maid is gone...

CHAPTER SIX

WHAT FLAG ARE YOU FLYING TODAY?

Q. was fixing breakfast for the cats, and Ying-Tong sat watching him, tapping the floor with the black tip of her silver tail. Poon-Tang was on the second-floor bookshelves somewhere, knocking things over.

The second floor wasn't really a floor at all—but a wooden perimeter with flooring and rails which held bookcases on all four sides. In this regard, the place looked like an old-fashioned library. Two exposed beams ran across the length of the whole barn—and down below were the various regions in which Q. lived his solitary bachelor life: the tiny bedroom, the cherrywood table with the computer, the oak writing desk (where he did no writing at all), and the old tweed couch—nearly shredded now by the cats—which was everybody's favorite place to work or eat or deliciously squander time.

By now the eggs had cooked for a minute. Q. covered them with grated Gruyere cheese and then poured hot cream over the top. Ying-Tong thumped her tail more rapidly now—even she knew the recipe. Q. took the covered eggs in their ramekin and placed it in a pan of hot water—then baked it until the cheese had melted.

He was placing the hot fragrant eggs into the cats' bowls when he heard the double-ring of a bicycle bell.

Through the curtains he saw Sallybikerun come sailing up the driveway. She was looking vibrantly summery. Sallybikerun was her screen-name, and Q. was so enchanted with it that he frequently called her that. She was attending Dartmouth College—had just finished her sophomore year—but during the summer and holidays worked for Q.—his amanuensis, she liked to say, a much more exotic-sounding word than gal-Friday. She also worked at the Big-Ass Bike Shop on South Avenue: a store that specialized in bikes for middle-aged customers. "We've got two kinds of bikes," Sally liked to say. "Bikes for people with big asses, and bikes for people with *really* big asses." She was nearly always smiling—she had brown hair cut as short as a guy's—and had this spunky tomboy quality that Q. fell instantly in love with.

Today she was dressed in lime-green shorts with matching lime-green sunglasses and an orange *They Might Be Giants* tee-shirt.

"Hey, you old fart," she said, entering the back door. (She had her own keys.) "I got you a green tea from the diner. Vicki says she's still in love with you."

"What flag are you flying today?"

She thought a second, then took a glance down her shorts. "Indians." She wobbled her palm in front of her mouth in an Indian war-whoop—and laughed at her own childishness.

"Indians *are* dangerous," he said. "So it's appropriate."

"Very dangerous." She did the tomahawk chop.

Sallybikerun had a boyfriend-thing going on with both

the mechanics at the Big-Ass Bike Shop: Steve and Eddie—and they were the ones who used to flirt with her by asking what flag she was flying today—meaning: what was printed on her boxers? She'd told all this to Q. last year, and had explained that "it's all innocent."

"Watch out," Q. had said. "When any mechanic asks you about your underwear, he's got more on his mind than just adjusting your gears."

Anyway, the relationships with Steve and Eddie had become fairly explicit, and she had managed so far to keep either one from knowing about the other. This balancing of secret boyfriends, her parents, and work had compelled Q. to finally award her with the adjective *dangerous*. She reciprocated by bestowing on him the adjective *gentle*—but it didn't seem nearly so appropriate.

"Be careful," was Q's only piece of fatherly advice. "Don't wind up pregnant or diseased. It isn't worth it for these two."

"I know," she had said. "I'm just having fun."

"It's not love?"

She shook her head. "They're my boy-toys. My boyfriends *du jour*. You know, I bike, I run, I've got my hair cut so short. People might think I'm a lesbian. So I keep Steve and Eddie to confirm my hetero status."

"Be careful, Sallybikerun."

She laughed. "I'm twenty. At twenty you're not supposed to be careful. I should tell you some of the stuff that happened in Paris."

She'd been there earlier in the summer to watch the

end of the Tours de France.

"I don't think I could handle it this early in the morning."

"I was thinking of writing a porno novel about it. The hero would be this American girl studying in Paris."

"Really?"

"I've got the title: 'Sore Bone Summer.'"

An hour later Sally was going through his fan letters and the speaking offers from elementary school librarians. And the foreign royalty statements and the rest of the paper-trail generated by a low-level success. She had the radio pouring out old soul classics on Felix Hernandez's "Rhythm Revue," and she was singing along with Edwin Starr's "Twenty Five Miles"—counting down how many miles he had to go. She was practically dancing in her chair when she answered the phone.

"Earl Bettinger," she said aloud—turning to Q.

He rolled his eyes.

"Can I take a message?"

On the corkboard facing the desk she had tacked a Polaroid of herself posing like the famous Janet Jackson *Rolling Stone* cover: wearing no shirt and covering her breasts with her palms.

She was writing on her pad—returned the phone to the cradle and turned to Q.

"He says he looked up 'lavender ink.' What's that?"

"A clue maybe."

"He says—" she looked at her notes—"Mary Astor's famous diary from the summer of 1936 was supposedly written in lavender ink."

"Mary Astor."

Q. was already heading up the stairs to the library.
"Who's that?"

"Did you ever see *The Maltese Falcon*?"

"No."

"I forgot. You're the generation that won't watch black and white movies."

"They all suck."

"*It's a Wonderful Life* sucks?"

"Well, it's no *American Pie 2*. Where did you get this?" she said. She was fingering a brass letter opener with a medallion welded to the handle.

"When you're a runner-up for the Newberry Award, but you don't actually win it, they give you that to remind you what a loser you are. I told my publisher they should put a sticker on the books: 'Newberry-Award-Losing...'"

Up on the second floor, Poon-Tang yowled and knocked a book off the shelf as he ran along the tops of them.

Q. picked it up: Howard Teichmann's *George S. Kaufman: An Intimate Memoir*. Things were strangely falling into place. "Good boy," he said.

Kaufman had written *June Moon* and, if Q. remembered correctly, had also appeared famously and scandalously in Mary Astor's diary.

He flipped through the photographs: there was Kaufman—tall, gangly, round eyeglasses, gigantic triangular nose—like Groucho playing Lincoln—and there was Mary Astor: the slinky little pug-nosed starlet—one of the great beauties of the period. That she was enthusiastically humping this high-octane-Hebe was nearly unbelievable (and certainly gave hope to the millions of others Gentile-fantasizers out there.) Her diary had exploded as one of the great lurid scandals of the Depression.

Sally was already searching the Internet downstairs. "This looks like pretty hot stuff," she said.

"It's right up there with 'Sore Bone Summer.'"

"Hey, that's my title!"

According to what they could glean from their resources, the diary had been leaked to the newspapers by Astor's husband, Dr. Franklyn Thorpe, when Astor brought a suit to contest their divorce. She wanted an annulment, award of the child, plus money and property. Thorpe countered with his own suit, alleging her wild promiscuity and entering into evidence her detailed sexual chronicle—written in her perfect schoolgirl penmanship. The encounters began in May of 1933—and soon she was writing of her "thrilling ecstasy" with the playwright George S. Kaufman. The period newspapers quoted at length her diary, practically licking their lips: "He fits me perfectly." She wrote of "exquisite moments... twenty, count them, diary, twenty... I don't see how he does it."

"Twenty!" said Sallybikerun. "The boyfriends *du jour* couldn't do twenty—and this guy looks like he's ninety."

As Q. looked down, the light from the venetian blinds falling in soft stripes formed a trapezoid on the floor, and now shifted into movement as the tree branches rose and fell in the breeze. He actually caught his breath at the scene's sudden startling beauty.

"Born Lucille Langhanke, in Quincy, Illinois," said Sally. "There's a real Hollywood name: Langhanke. Overbearing father. Recognized his daughter's beauty. We all know what that means. Entered her in Hollywood contest. Under the wing of John Barrymore. Affair with Barrymore while still a teenager. He's in his forties. Very sweet."

"Very Hollywood."

"Silent films. Sound films. And then, in the summer of 1936... oh, here's the diary stuff. Scandal of the decade. Worldwide headlines. Kaufman referred to as 'Public Lover Number One.' That's good. Explicit sexual liaison with the older married playwright, meticulously chronicled in her schoolgirl script in lavender ink!"

"And whatever happened to the diary?"

She scrolled rapidly through the pages. "Doesn't seem to say... Rumors that it was a forgery... Astor, in later years, said most of the excerpts published from it had been forged by journalists... Rumors that the diary was eventually burned..."

Meanwhile, upstairs, Q. had been flipping through the Teichmann book. "Look at this," he said. Leaning over the railing he read to her: "'The diary was not burned by court order, as was supported by the wire services, but is locked in the Managing Editor's Confidential File in a vault three levels under East 42nd Street in New York

City.' That was in—" He checked the copyright page. "1972."

"What do you think? Still there?"

"I don't know. *The Daily News* is not on 42nd Street anymore, I don't think."

"It's on 33rd Street," she said. "There's an all-night diner down there. The Cheyenne. I know exactly where it is. Steve takes me there when we're out in the city, and everything else is closed. There's a good bike shop around the block, too."

"You want to go down there and investigate?"

She laughed. "What exactly am I investigating?"

"Whether or not the diary still exists?"

"And who do I say I am?"

"You say you're writing a book on Mary Astor."

"Oh, yeah, I really look like I'm an author."

"Every door in the place will be open to you because you're good looking."

"Right."

"You don't understand the way guys operate, Sally. Cute opens every door; every lock. A plucky pretty girl can get anything she wants in this world. We live in a world *entirely* based on appearances."

"I don't believe that."

"You think if Princess Di had been cross-eyed and had funny teeth that five thousand people would have shown up for her funeral?"

"So what are you saying?"

"I'm saying that if *you* show up—looking just like you

do: shorts, sneakers, and a tee-shirt with the sleeves rolled up, you'll get in to see the editor in chief. And that if *I* showed up—a goofy-looking middle-aged fart, I wouldn't make it past the receptionist. Do you really think I'm wrong?"

She thought a moment. The light still shifted and undulated around her.

"No, you're probably right," she said. "It's not fair, but it's true. But I'm not showing up cold."

"I'll meet you there, if you like—but *you* have to be there."

"And suppose I find the diary? What does that prove? What do I do with it? What am I looking for?"

"Sally, my dear," said Q. "That's the *mystery*."

CHAPTER SEVEN

THE MOTHER AND CHILD REUNION

Q. left Sallybikerun to complete what research he could, and he found himself food shopping in Trader Joe's where he paid exorbitant prices for red organic grapes and bottled carrot juice in the hopeful notion that it might neutralize the extra-fatty corned beef sandwich he'd eaten an hour earlier. He imagined the dialogue within his stomach:

"Jesus Christ, he eats the entire sandwich. And not even lean yet. All right, stomach cancer, let's roll."

"No, no, no—look at what he paid for those organic grapes. Lousy grapes, too—soft ones."

"Kiss my ass, five grapes don't balance out sixteen ounces of nitrate-soaked beef. *Somebody's* paying for this."

"Hey, man, carrot juice, anti-oxidant, beta-caratene. Come on, give him a break. He's *trying*."

"Trying? Mr. Brown Rice Snaps—followed by a dark Dove bar? This is like the woman who orders 'herbal tea—no sugar' in the restaurant so her friends can see how disciplined she is, and then goes home and eats an entire Entenmann's coffee cake."

All the debit-card machines were down; he rooted around for the cash.

The woman behind him said: "Mr. Qafka?"

He turned.

She was a well turned-out woman in her late thirties: sunglasses and a stylish white scarf around her hair.

"I'm Hilary Olsen."

He shook his head automatically, but he registered no recognition except her perfume—which was far from delicate and evocative of someone else.

"What a surprise running into you like this," she said.

"Yes."

"I'm Gwen Duveen's mother. And Jesse's."

"Oh, right. Of course."

He must have met her at some school function promoting the writing program. His Creative Writing seminar was, apparently, the jewel in the crown of the high school English offerings, and parents lobbied to get their children enrolled.

Her hand was warm, and she lowered her voice.

"Gwen *adored* the class."

"I'm pleased."

"Of course, she wouldn't show me a thing she wrote because, Lord knows, I'm her mother, and you just don't do that."

"It was impressive stuff. Very original. Unique. Funny."

He had no memory of a single word she had written. He remembered her blue sailor shirt and Brad, the big tanned lunk of a boyfriend who rendezvoused with her everyday at the end of class. Q. would look at them leaving together and wonder whose house they went to—and how much elapsed time would pass before her brassiere hit the floor. *B minus 58 minutes.*

"...She said it really inspired her, and that she looked at writing in a whole new way."

"I'm glad," he said, and he saw she was checking out just a six-pack of Volvic bottled water—the useless debit card in her hand. She had the same long-fingered, slender hands as her daughter.

"God knows when the machines will be running here, Mrs. Olsen," Q. said. "I've got a ton of cash; let me pay for the water."

"No—really—"

"Come on. Let me be a big sport for five dollars."

"Then I insist I pay you back."

He gallantly paid for her water, and they walked out to the parking lot together. The heat and humidity were rising unpleasantly—but she was a pretty and amiable companion—and Q. looked at her—telling of Gwen's cooking lessons and her boy's trumpet lessons and baseball games ("You think it's going to be *less* running around in the summer, but, believe me, it's *more*.") and he thought what charmed lives these Westfield women lead: orthodontists and designer sneakers and perfume—all held aloft on the currents of their husbands' immaculately air-conditioned Wall Street thievery. It was a life of ludicrous privilege—but at least, he thought, the privilege turned its flowered fruit towards the children—offering them every possible choice and enrichment—and if her careful little girl was being nailed right now on the kitchen table by a sweaty, condomless lacrosse player, the heirloom drinking glasses (Depression glass!) smashing onto the floor—well, girls will be girls...

She thanked him again.

He moved nimbly to the driver's side of his peanut butter-colored Checker Marathon—the black plastic seats blazing, and turned the key to make a well-choreographed exit.

Which was fine except the car wouldn't start. Not only wouldn't start, but wouldn't make a click.

Totally dead.

He cursed. Opened the hood in the absurd way suburbanites did—as if a liberal arts degree might somehow help you repair an internal combustion engine.

"Oh, dear."

Mrs. Olsen had walked back towards him.

"Dear man, let me give you a lift."

His wounded car was dragged by its teeth to the gas station across the street on Elm. They couldn't even look at it for an hour.

Hilary Olsen volunteered to drive Q. to her house on Tremont Avenue—and have the station call there.

"I have to pick up Gwen at Chez Catherine anyhow."

And so, a little awkwardly and, maybe, a little guiltily, he found himself sitting in the Duveen kitchen—as white and spotless as a hospital—as Hilary Olsen served him wet Washington State cherries.

"I really feel I'm imposing," Q. said.

"Not at all. I'm honored to have a great writer in my house."

"Please."

"Listen. You were once Harold's client. It's the least I can do."

They made some small talk about his investigation of the death of Lilian Jackson Braun; about the mysterious diary. She listened with polite disinterest.

There was a photograph of Gwen on the refrigerator wearing her French sailor's shirt sitting on the sand, leaning against a yellow sailboat, her head tilted to the right, the setting sun filling the right side of each footprint with shadow.

"Do you think she's pretty?" asked Mrs. Olsen.

"Oh, I don't know. I don't notice much about the students I teach. I concentrate on the work. But it's a beautiful photograph, the composition: the blue sky, the darker blue water, the vertical line of the sailboat and ropes. I don't know what I'm talking about really."

"I think she's beautiful. Strikingly beautiful. But maybe all mothers think that. Quasimodo's mother probably thought that. Gwen's an unpleasant child, but a remarkably good-looking one. The looks she gets from her father—and, now that I think of it, maybe the unpleasantness, too."

"She seemed very—what's the word?—*poised* to me."

"*That* I'll take credit for."

"You're modest. She gets the looks from you, too."

Hilary smiled. Ate another cherry. Wiped her fingers with a napkin. "It's hot in here," she said. "I'm sorry. We have a service contract for the air conditioning, but they can't get here till tomorrow."

"It's not too bad," Q. said.

"It's dreadful. I feel like I'm going to pass out."

"I hadn't even noticed actually. You're supposed to notice things as a writer. But I seem to be in a fog most of the time."

She was at the sink, letting cold water run across her wrists. "You don't have to be a writer to be living in a fog."

"I suppose not."

She was hardly talking to Q.—looking out the window. "You could be a suburban housewife, whatever the hell that means. You could come home each day to a spoiled, selfish daughter who flaunts her sexual activity in your face."

"I don't see any pictures of Harold here."

"Look," she said, turning around to Q. and taking off her scarf. "I can't stand this heat. I can't breathe. I'm going up to Gwen's room—at least she's got a wall unit. Please come up. This is ridiculous. There's a phone up there. You can call about your car."

She had moved out of the kitchen and was heading up the back staircase.

Q. called up the stairs. "Isn't Gwen going to mind if we're up in her room?"

"Gwen's not coming home tonight," said her retreating voice, moving up the stairs. "I just remembered. And neither is her brother."

Q. stood there staring at a white wooden newel post.

"And Harold won't be home either. This is Tuesday. That's the night he fucks Stacey."

"This air conditioner is from the Stone Age," she said, bending down to raise the thermostat. She was wearing a black sleeveless shirt—a silver watch on her right wrist. Her slacks seemed to be made of olive silk—no socks—and black heels. The air conditioner had been installed low on the floor, and her hair (blondish brown) hung freely and loosely as she bent her neck to find the dials. He could see the line of her underwear through the olive slacks.

She turned towards him: her eyes jade-colored like Gwen's. Her face round as the moon and pale and intelligent and angry.

She held up her right palm, and the edge of it was streaked with grease. "I tried to replace the belt myself on the central air. *That* was fun."

"Do you want me to try? I'm pretty handy with tools."

Her cell phone beeped, and she took it from her silk pocket. Her arms looked strong, and Q. imagined she spent her mornings working out.

"Hi, Stacey," she said. She sat on the edge of Gwen's bed.

Q. sat in a little green wooden chair at the make-up table. He was afraid it might crack under his weight.

"Good. Thanks for letting me know."

She moved her hair behind her ear and placed the phone down on the quilt.

"Not the gas station I take it?"

She smiled a little painfully. "Stacey. Harold's secretary."

Q. nodded meaninglessly.

"Like I told you. It's Tuesday night. So while I'm watching Larry King, I can rest easy knowing that they're fucking at the Algonquin. I'm not asking for your reaction, in fact, I don't want your reaction; I'm just telling you the facts." She wiped her brow. "This air conditioner makes no fucking difference. God, I'm boiling. Why don't you take the hat off, sir? And the coat off? We're going to be here an hour or so."

Gwen's perfume was overpowering in the room. The whole room was done in pale blues and whites—a canopy bed with white posts. Her blue-striped sailor shirt lay on the bed. On the wall by the make-up table were photographs: Shirtless Brad and shirtless male friends spelling B-L-U-E D-E-V-I-L-S; Gwen in a cranberry-colored formal gown, Gwen in a bikini sitting aloft Brad's shoulders as he stood in what looked like a hot tub.

"The perfume is so strong here; I don't know how she doesn't get a headache," Q. said.

"Yes, I'm sorry... My mother used to say to me: 'Hilary, how can you have a headache when you don't have a head?' I suppose the modern equivalent of that is: 'Gwen, how can you have a headache when you're out giving head?'"

"Please."

"Not *poised* enough for you?"

"It's just none of my business." Q. looked longingly

towards the door.

"Here's something that's your business."

She reached an arm through the sunlight pouring through the curtains and retrieved a thick spiral school notebook. "You know what this is?"

She flipped through pages—heavy with ink.

"It looks like her Creative Writing journal."

"Did you ever read it?"

"No. I encourage them to keep a journal, but I don't collect it. I tell them it's none of my business."

"Good for you. I admire your restraint. Let me ask you something? If you were a teenaged girl and kept a private journal, would you keep it here on your nightstand in the open?" She gestured with her eyes to the table.

"Probably not."

"Why?" Her voice was tight and short—and Q. thought: *This woman is an emotional landmine.*

"I'd probably be afraid—"

"—your parents would find it, and read it. Of course you would. You'd hide it in a drawer. Find *some* place in this room out of sight. Anybody would." She smiled. "So why does my daughter leave it out here? *Every* day. By the side of her bed." She was flipping through its pages. "I'll save you the trouble of answering." She plucked from her pocket a pair of black-rimmed reading glasses.

And then she read in an emotionless voice:

"'My mother is such a bitch. Bitch. Bitch. Bitch. I fucking hate her guts. She is miserable and feels she has to take it out on me. I cannot do *anything* right. The other night I tell her I'm going out to Brad's. She fucking goes ballistic. She tells me I'm never home, that I'm using the house as a hotel. I tell her, Why should I stay here and listen to you bellyache about what a shitty life you have. You married the stupid fuck. Then she tells me that she's not going to divorce him until Jesse's through with high school, which is like another four years. I said, Good. Be miserable for four more years because you're too weak to leave him. She *exploded*. She told me she hated me and that I ruined her life. I told her I was spending the night at Brad's. She said, Good. Go get yourself knocked up again. This time I exploded. Fuck you! You know you can't stand me because I'm sexually active and you're a desperate dried up old cunt at 39. I hate her. I hate her. I hate her.'" Hilary's voice was breaking now in both anger and tears. But she continued to read: "'She's weak. I swear to God and make a vow that if I ever turn out like her I'll kill myself.'"

Q. raised his hand in a gesture of compassion, but she stopped him.

"There's more. 'So I went over to Brad's and he was in a shitty mood which was just what I didn't need. People came over and I ended up getting so wasted. At one point it was like 2 in the morning and I was in the hot tub in just my bra and underwear with Brad and Mike L. who were just in their boxers and I was so fucking drunk that I blew them both as they sat on the tiles and I stood in the water. It was fucking sick and disgusting and I felt like the biggest slut and I couldn't believe what I was doing and I couldn't believe Brad wanted me to do this. I'm supposed to be his girlfriend, right? But I was drunk and angry and I kept thinking, This one's for you, Mom.'"

She put down the journal. She was shaking.

"This is what my daughter writes about. And this is what she leaves for me to find. Leaves it open to that page across the middle of her bed."

"I'm sorry," Q. said. "But she's a teenager, Hilary. You have to remember that. I work with these kids. They're not particularly nice to you or anybody else. To you these are words that are going to hurt for a lifetime; to Gwen, it's blowing off steam for five minutes in a journal. Next week she won't even remember it."

"She left this *out* for me to find, James."

"She wanted to hurt you."

Hilary stood up.

"I want to hurt her back."

"Hilary, I don't want to get in the middle of this."

"Do you want to fuck my daughter?"

"What?"

"I said: Do you want to fuck my daughter?"

"Absolutely not." Q. was backing away now.

Hilary closed the bedroom door, and took Gwen's sailor shirt off the bed.

Then she was unbuttoning her black sleeveless blouse.

It felt as if it were one hundred and fifty degrees in that room. It may have been. The air conditioner did nothing except make noise.

"Hilary, please."

She was topless now except for a small gray silk brassiere. She slipped on Gwen's sailor's shirt.

"I'm Gwen and you're Brad. And I want you to fuck me like you've been waiting for it for nineteen years."

She took off her glasses.

Q. turned to her: her perfume, her striped shirt.

"I want it," she said. "Now."

And he thought to himself: *What the hell...*

She held Q.'s head clamped between her legs. Her fingers bit into his hair and she was genuinely hurting him.

"Bradley!" she was crying out. "You're eating me out! Brad! Brad!" With each groan of the name she shifted her torso.

Q. was thinking to himself that if he left this session with any of his front teeth left it would be a small miracle. And while she was thrashing about, he wondered what he'd say to the dentist to explain how his two front teeth got knocked in.

He finally looked up. "Are we anywhere near the jackpot?"

"Fuck me up the ass, Brad," she said. "I'll come like that." She snapped her fingers.

"Damn it, Bradley! I can't believe you're fucking me up the a—God damn it, Bradley!

They were slicked in sweat.

"Are we almost there, Gwen?"

"Almost. You can work a little harder."

Yeah, thought Q, and work my way right into the Cardiac Unit.

"You're in such good shape," Q. said, admiring her back and shoulders.

"All buffed up and no one to fuck. Come *on*, now."

She had a small black tattoo on her shoulder blade. It was an animal of some type.

He touched it. "I didn't think you were the tattoo type."

"It was a sorority thing," she said.

"It looks like an armadillo."

"Just shut up, Brad."

The cell phone rang, and in one millisecond she had removed herself from his meat thermometer and was speaking in perfectly composed tones on the phone.

He lay there on his back: sore, exhausted, dehydrated, a beached dolphin gulping for air.

"Yes, this is Mrs. Olsen. Yes, the Checker... May I take a message?... OK, not ready until noon tomorrow at the earliest providing you can get the part... Really? I'll have to check into that. Thank you!"

She turned off the phone.

"I want you to make me feel like a little girl," she said. She was naked except for the striped shirt.

"What?"

"I want you to make me feel like a teenage girl."

"I'm shot," he said. "I'm sorry."

"Hold on," she said—and she was swinging off the bed.

"What?"

She whispered: "I want you to shave my pussy."

Now a disposable Trac II razor may be fine for smoothing out a day's growth of whiskers—maybe even two days—but it was never designed to mow down thirty nine years of industrial-strength muff.

It clogged.

It choked on shaving cream and hair.

"Do you like this?" she kept asking. "Do you like doing this?"

"Oh, yeah," he said.

It was one of the most ludicrous, degrading, hopeless tasks he had ever been asked to perform.

The bed was full of shaving-cream-and-hair-soaked Kleenex, as he tried desperately to unclog the razor.

"I don't think this is working, Gwen."

"This is making me *so* hot!"

And, finally, his water-soaked boxers around his ankles, he sat naked on the tiles which lined the square bathtub. Mrs. Olsen was kneeling in the water—in her daughter's bra and underwear. She was licking his dick with all the emotion of a high-speed robot in an automated Honda factory.

"Say it again," she said.

"Do I have to?"

"I'll stop if you don't."

"Gwen, I want you to blow us both."

"That is sick and disgusting."

"Come on, Gwen."

"You're supposed to be my boyfriend."

"This'll be fun."

"This is gross. Say: 'Do it, bitch.'"

"Do it, bitch."

"This one's for you, mom," she said.

And at that point, Q. finally found a half-hearted, dribbling release.

"This one's for you, mom," she continued—and she was suddenly sobbing against his legs.

"God, what's wrong with me?" she said. "Please, God, tell me what's wrong with me?" Her eyes were closed.

What he said was: "You're fine, Hilary."

What he thought was: *You are the sickest fuck I ever met.*

CHAPTER EIGHT

BE SCARED

"Got any enemies?"

Dion, the mechanic at the Elm Street Gulf—a wise-ass kid in his mid-twenties—stepped out of the back holding a length of wires. "Seven different cables replaced. Two of them we could have spliced, but they're never the same, and comes the winter, you don't want the car not starting, so we replaced them all."

Q. said: "How can seven wires go bad at the same time?"

"Nothing went bad." He held out a red lead severed neatly before the connector. "Cut. All of them. Like I said: Got any enemies?" Dion did his Bugs Bunny voice: "It's saba-toojie, doc."

Q. stopped at the library on the way home, for no other reason than he felt drawn there. In the mystery section stood a row of orange and red covers: the Lilian Jackson Braun series. He rubbed his hand along the spines and wondered if the answer was in there somewhere. *The answer?* he thought. What the hell is the question? There was the whole well-thumbed collection: *The Cat Who Called A Spayed a Spade*; *The Cat Who Smelled Like a Pussy*. He picked one at random and opened it to the dedication: "To Harold Duveen: the best lawyer Green

Stamps can buy..."

An unpleasant coincidence.

And he wondered what on earth poor Hilary Olsen had ever seen in Harold Duveen? OK, the woman was psychotic, a Freudian freakjob of case-study proportions, but still... Harold Duveen? Formerly Harold Duvlopkin. As Roth liked to say, he was the kind of Jew who justified anti-Semitism: loud, self-satisfied, the tinted eyeglasses, and the Parliaments. Q. remembered a scene they shared once in a Thai restaurant—Duveen had started in immediately:

"Is this the only round table in the non-smoking section?"

It was right from the Jackie Mason routine.

Then he asked about a beer.

"We have many kind Thai beer," said the acquiescent waiter.

"No, no. What *American* beer have you got?"

Ten minute discussion on that—and, finally, the waiter brings him a frosted mug and a beer bottle.

"No, no." Duveen's head was shaking. "I want a *normal* glass. A room temperature glass."

Q. was shrinking into his chair.

And this was the schmuck Hilary Olsen had married. Hilary who had gone to Princeton!

She was Duveen's second wife. Q. had known the first wife, too—Hannah—a yenta with red nails who was physically unable to pick up a container of food without looking at the fat content. "You know why I left her?" Duveen had said once to Q. "Because she always looked like she was smelling shit."

Q. thought about his chance meeting with Hilary in Trader Joe's.

He also remembered seeing her jogging a few times around the track in Tamaques Park. He wrote sometimes in that park—sitting at an old picnic table, the crickets trilling. Q. had grown up in that park—could still feel his childhood tangibly around him there—and when the writing flagged, he walked to the tree where his father had once carved his initials. The tree's growth had distorted it over the last forty-five years, but there is was: JQ. The letters were now wide and weird. And there, a few trees away, was JQ + VJD—a high-school romance thinning and stretching with thirty-three years.

He was sitting in the magazine section of the library now—staring, unseeing, at the magazine titles he would never in his life read: *American Cheerleader*, *Car and Driver*—when he was startled by a tap on his shoulder.

It was Hilary Olsen.

"Long time, no see."

She touched his arm. "We've got to stop meeting like this. I think Harold is getting suspicious." She laughed.

She was wearing Gwen's perfume again. Her blonde hair was pulled back in a ponytail today; she wore stylish round reading glasses, blue denim shorts, and a gray tee-shirt that read "Ocean Gate."

"I just wanted to say," she began, "that I enjoyed myself terribly yesterday. I hope I didn't embarrass you. I know it was a little out there, but that's what I think good sex is: you take this wild free-fall and the other person is there to catch you, right? It was *recreational*, James. All right? That's all it was. If it happens again, great. If it never does, then we had a memorable afternoon?" She smiled warmly at him. "Don't think about it too much, all right? And please, dear God, don't use it in one of your books. *Promise* me that."

"Word of honor."

He noticed the pale remnants of the grease stain still on her palm.

"Did the air conditioner guy ever show up?"

"He's coming sometime between noon and four—I have to get back. Later!"

She was already leaving with her two books and her videotape.

It was one of those moments when you realize you've been seeing the entire universe incorrectly.

Q. was holding onto the railing tightly. Somebody said hello. Q.'s eyes were somewhere else.

He wandered out onto Stanley Avenue—turned right towards Lenox.

Mrs. Hilary Olsen.

Of the tiny silver watch.

And the olive silk pants.

He saw, in his mind's eye, the grease on her palm.

It hadn't come from trying to fix the air conditioner. It had come from the engine of his car.

The Checker was old enough that you could release the hood without access to the inside of the car.

She'd seen—no, she'd *followed* him to Trader Joe's.

She'd watched him from inside her red Saturn—he imagined that face behind the windshield—sunglasses, scarf—and she'd waited until he was in the store—and, God, this took nerve and speed—she'd run out with wire cutters in her hand—brazenly opened the hood of his car. And who would have stopped her? Or even questioned her? People didn't do that. Certainly not in Westfield.

Snip. Snip. Snip.

The whole thing could have taken half a minute.

But a hand rubs against a hose or the battery or the alternator and picks up a line of grease.

The clippers go where? Not her car because they might be seen by Q. Not even in the trunk. No. Into her pocketbook, he thought.

And then in she goes to Trader Joe's—watching him between the organic baby greens and the caramel-blast powerbars, waiting, waiting—and then eases just behind him in line with her Volvic waterbottles.

And is it coincidence that the debit machines are down?

Oh, she times it well. The parking lot. The twenty steps towards her own car. The concerned cross-over, twenty steps back to his.

Why?

To get revenge on her brutal little daughter?

Christ, none of it had been an accident.

The encounters while she was jogging.

She was following him. Clearly this had been going on for awhile.

He thought of the words he'd heard Stumpy Rabinowitz say in the diner—a certain lady was interested in a certain celebrated children's book writer. Hilary Olsen was stalking him? OK, too strong a word. *Scoping* him?

Maybe he should be flattered. A pretty woman interested in him. OK, a sick, mentally-ill woman...but a *pretty* mentally-ill woman.

And she was still following him. Was he supposed to believe that this meeting in the reference section of the library at 11:30 in the morning was a coincidence?

A voice deep in his solar plexus said: "Be scared, James. Be very scared."

CHAPTER NINE

SPICE GIRL

Sallybikerun arose from the escalator at Penn Station into the bright noise of New York. She caught a wavering glimpse of herself in a window and was pleased. Most days she actually liked her body. It was, as the affirmation tape she ran with said, her perfect servant.

She was about as dressed up as she could handle for a ninety-degree day in the city. An orange tanktop, khaki shorts, and dress sneakers. (Giving up her flip-flops required real courage.)

As the doors opened, she could feel the heat of the city pressing in, hear the sirens, and she smiled as she stepped out onto the sidewalk—the entire city honeycombed with sweet *possibility*.

And, perhaps, what pleased her even more was that this was *her* chapter. For once she simply wasn't making witty comebacks for Q., but the camera was in *her* head this time. She could go into bike stores, and listen to her music on the Walkman. And why not? she thought. I'm funny; I'm lively; I'm observant—what had Q. called her: *peppery!* She laughed aloud. That was a cool word—no one but he would have thought of it. And she liked to think of herself as a little peppery. The spice girl.

She had almost an hour until her appointment at *The*

Daily News (on 33rd Street—right around the corner) so she bought herself a smoothie at Lenny Juice: a 1950's-type juice bar with a life-sized cutout of comedian Lenny Bruce on the sidewalk giving the finger and Bruce monologues blaring from the speakers inside. ("Tits and ass!" "What did you say?" "I said tits and ass." "Well, you can't just put 'Tits and Ass' up on the marquis." "OK, how about American tits and ass? Grandma Moses's tits and Norman Rockwell's ass?")

She was drinking a carrot and beet and wheatgrass.

The guy behind her ordered: "One large Blah-Blah-Blah—extra ginger. And a decaf Tuchis Lecker."

A building across the street was covered in a tawdry video screen, and she tried to avoid looking at it. It felt like visual pollution.

Instead, she tried to concentrate on her own body. To actually feel it. She believed in her body. At Westfield High School she'd started the Outdoors Club, and at Dartmouth she rowed and biked and ran track (despite her asthma.) Last fall she'd even tried throwing the discus! She often visualized her body as pure light and energy—even at rest: spinning, spinning—right down to the molecular level. She only really forgot herself, or at least forgot self-consciousness, engaged in something deeply physical. Even her so-called "dangerous" sex life was an attempt to forget herself—and maybe that was its most pleasing aspect.

Around the corner from the Cheyenne Diner, she walked into a bike store called Disraeli Gears.

"Hey," said a punked-out guy with dyed golden hair behind the counter. He had been reading the Lance Armstrong book. He studied Sally for a second—then asked: "Road bike or mountain bike?"

"Both," said Sally, and thought to herself that *both* described her essential take on life.

The guy said: "You spend somewhere around two grand on a road bike, and you can get something around seventeen and a half pounds..."

"Full Shimano Ultegra components?" asked Sally, all innocence.

The guy raised an eyebrow and smiled.

She smiled.

Another victory.

She puttered around the store, and the smell of the place reminded her of the boyfriends *du jour:* Steve and Eddie.

Eddie was the easy one to explain—he looked a little like the guy behind the counter here—like most guys in a bikeshop—a little too nerdy, a little too solitary, a little too thin, and a little too horny—but decent and shy and hopelessly serious: his hair falling in his eyes, his black shirt. It took him an entire month to kiss her—it was really kind of sweet. He sent her lengthy e-mails about the nature of their relationship. If she yawned when they were together she got a two-page single-spaced self-punishing rant on how "I know I'm not interesting enough for you." She was the sexual initiator always—and he was so stunned, so grateful, and so determined to even out the score of physical pleasure that he *labored* over her.

At twenty-nine, he lived with his parents, and she was living at home all summer, so their romantic assignations took place at an abandoned bench they found in the middle of Brightwood Park. Her primary memory of the park was how hot it was—like a rainforest—and she liked to close her eyes, on her back on the bench, her sports bra jammed above her small breasts, and listen to the crows calling to each other, as he worked and worked until his wrist probably felt like terminal arthritis had set in.

Unfortunately, the only way for her to achieve some kind of sexual release was to imagine him as someone else—almost anyone else.

And after twenty-seven minutes of grunting labor to get her relaxed, she'd turn to him, and twenty-seven seconds later he was done.

Then he'd take her out to eat.

"...a carbon fiber fork, and cool wheelset," said the clerk.

"Mavic Ksryium wheels?"

"Exactly."

Steve, however, was something else. Girls called him Steevil. Smaller, tougher, like a well-built soccer player with a tiny Mephistophelian goatee, he was an ostentatious womanizer: middle-schoolers, mothers, daughters, grandmothers, goats—it made no difference—he was an insatiable satyr: a liar and a charmer whose sexual universe contained an infinite number of black holes. He was a diminutive, red-faced salesman of randiness: "Sally, you are *not* letting me go home like *this*."

"Steve, I'm exhausted."

"Hey, I worked for fifty-two minutes on you. Fifty-two minutes, I checked."

"I didn't come."

"I can't help it if getting you to come is like climbing Mount Olympus. I tried, damn it. I lived up to my part of the contract."

"Contract?"

"Damn straight, contract." He was standing in her parents' basement, leaning against the pool table in his heather-colored boxers, his glistening satellite receiver raised to receive premium programming.

"Steve, I feel like I'm going to throw up."

"Well, there's no way I'm going home like this. Look, if you can't help me I'm going to march upstairs and say, 'Mrs. Corcoran, is there anyway you can help me with this thing?' And if that doesn't work let's get your little sister Jenna down here. 'Jen, I want to teach you something that's going to be very valuable to you later on in life. Now I know you've eaten an ice cream cone before, right?'"

"...Hayes hydraulic disc brakes, composite seat and chain stays..."

That was the thing about Steve—he was funny. He never pretended to be anything he wasn't. And while the summer had started with Steve as her boy-toy—he was, quite against her will, beginning to slip under her heart. He was only going to hurt her, disappoint her, betray her—kill her with irresponsibility—but there it was. She saw him all day in her head. She dialed his number on the cradled phone. It was his voice she heard calling her name in the silence between tracks on her CD. It would be Steve who called tonight at ten to ask her how her day in New York went and how he missed her at the shop and could they go out for a cup of coffee—which was code for: Will you give me a handjob in the car?

Poor guy. That's all he wanted.

Release. She felt a little sorry for him—his need to be loved was so bottomless—not only physically, but psychologically like some terrible performer coming out to milk fifty curtain calls, Steve needed more. Do you love me? *Yes.* How much do you love me! *More!*

"I bought a titanium frame last summer," said Sally. "And built it up with a set of XT and XTR components."

"Are you, like, dating anyone at the moment?" asked the guy. "I know this is really forward."

"No, not at the moment," she said.

She got his phone number.

In front of *The Daily News* building on 33rd Street—which looked, to Sally, like an inverted funnel, she could see Q. waiting for her; he was right on time as usual. A three-piece jazz combo (guitar, bass, drum-machine) was playing for tips on the street. She smiled at Q's slightly ridiculous outfit: the Panama hat, the white sports jacket, the lavender cravat, the luxuriant mustache, his black walking stick with the white tips that looked as if he should be dancing in an old musical.

He saluted her in mock formality, and she giggled.

Being the amanuensis to a slightly celebrated writer was probably the best job she'd ever had. Certainly the most fun. He made her laugh. He taught her things. And with Polly Thompson in Paris, she felt she'd taken on the female lead in his life's drama: the one who adjusted his suspenders and told him the pink shirt didn't go with the orange tie.

Steve and Eddie both didn't like him—bristling with a deep masculine jealousy. They insisted Q. was in love with her, despite the thirty-year difference—but Sally didn't care really what they thought. She got a good vibe out of the relationship, and if there was a little flirtatious energy in the air, well, so what? Nobody had any intention of acting on it. It was like John Steed and Mrs. Peel! The sparks were like the oxygen that made you see the world more clearly—black coffee that burned the dust off the circuits of your brain. And if there were mixed motives, so what? Q. had a quotation he'd cut from *The Provincetown Banner* tacked to the corkboard over his writing desk—from an interview with Norman Mailer. One afternoon, when Q. was out, Sally had copied it down: "Whatever you do, if it works out fairly well, you're not only doing it for your good motives but also for your bad motives. The greatest energy that you'll ever have, the most sizable energy that you have, is when your best motives and your worst motives are being satisfied."

She thought it was true in her relationships with both Steve and Eddie. There was the sort of scummy motive of gathering around her a lot of sexual opportunity, and having two guys admiring her, and the sinister playfulness of keeping them both in the dark about each other—despite that they worked in the same store. She'd given a hand-job to Eddie in the repair room in the back—and an hour later, when Eddie had gone to lunch, she'd done the exact same thing in the exact same place to Steve. And, OK, part of her felt like Bike Slut Number One (what her roommate Dominique at Dartmouth affectionately called her)—but part of her thought it was really funny—and even, in a crazy way, *loving*. (This was the good motive.) She liked them both, she genuinely did—didn't love either of them—but felt she had something to give both of them. Poor tall trembling pale Eddie: "I can't *believe* you're doing this, Sally" and then hotblooded red-faced Steve: "Damn, now *this* is what I call a lube-job." And it was more than just a happy little shot into a red rag smelling of Schwinn oil—she was saying to two guys who really needed it: a young good-looking girl likes your body. A young good-looking girl *wants* to do this. She felt like some slightly off-center incarnation of a flower-child. It was exhilarating in a modestly criminal way—and it was definitely, as Mailer said, her best and worst motives in fantastic fusion.

And here was Q. waiting for her—another guy in her life. But this relationship felt more like two kids in a club-house. There really was something childlike in Q., and it spoke to something childlike in her.

"Why, of all coincidences!" he said aloud. "Sallybikerun!"

She laughed at his theatrical silliness; she was glad to see him—but she realized, too, that her steering the chapter was over. Sally Corcoran would be Sallybikerun again—the charming bit player. But, she thought, I don't really mind. It was exhausting chronicling her inner life. It required a self-absorption and energy that she preferred channeling into biking or running.

"We're back in business," said Q. And the jazz combo on the street kicked into a jaunty melody from James Van Heusen's score of *Road to Utopia*.

Q. was about to sing.

"I didn't know this was a musical," said Sally. "Cool."

Q:	Like Sherlock Holmes and Watson,
	As they make their star debut,
	Put it there, Sal.
	Put it there.
SALLY:	We're up to chapter nine,
	And still we haven't got a clue.
	Put it there, pal.
	Put it there.
Q:	No secrets from each other!
	We'll solve this case, just watch.
	We'll soon be safe at home,
	With just the kitties and a Scotch.
SALLY:	At least this chapter hasn't seen you,
	Grabbing for your crotch!
Q:	For that, let's say a prayer.
BOTH:	Put it there!

The jazz combo played a tag, and Q. threw a few singles into the guitar case. Then they headed into the *News* building.

*   *   *

The senior managing editor of *The Daily News*, Albert Z. Carr, was taking the elevator with them down to the morgue and research room. "I'll show you the way," he said.

Carr's cell phone rang in the little victory fanfare that you heard at baseball games.

"Carr. Hi, honey. What did you hear?" He wiped his forehead. "The vaginal secretions are normal. See. I told you that. What did I tell you? What about the sores in your butt? ...Aloe. Right... I told you that, too. All right. Good news. Talk to you later. I love you."

He passed them into the morgue and research room which you entered through two walls of computer drives—noisy and hot. The room itself was just a long wooden table with one computer on it, and three walls of old filing cabinets—and two ancient microfilm readers. The room looked as if it had belonged to the old Soviet bureaucracy—a 1930's civil service office: green plastic seat cushions, plaster walls.

Carr left them with the custodian of the files, Sid Pannish. He was a roly-poly figure in his seventies: pants hitched astoundingly high; a washed-out, ribbed white short-sleeved shirt. He was soft-spoken with a thick New York accent.

"I'm a children's book writer," said Q. "This is Sally— Sarah Corcoran, my assistant.

"Well," he said, amused, "I'd like to see you get this stuff in a children's book."

"The diary is here."

"Where else would it be?"

"The rumors were that it was burned."

Pannish moved to the walk-in safe at the back of the room. "Been here since 1936," he said, tapping the safe. "I was fifteen years old. The old *News*. Joe Patterson's paper. That was a whole different New York. A civilized city. You can't imagine how alive it was. Times Square was like the center of the universe. It felt like New Year's Eve every night!" Pannish spun four numbers on the safe, and lugged open the iron door. Inside, Q. could see an old decal reading: *You are not locked in!*

Q. whispered to Sally: "He's one of these birds who's been down here his whole life. Every company has them. They usually smoke a pipe. Been down here with no windows wearing the same shirt for forty years." Q. raised his eyes to take in the hundreds of file drawers. "And if you want anything from these guys, you have to let 'em talk for ninety minutes."

Pannish emerged from the safe with what looked like an old inter-office envelope. He undid the twine fastener.

"A lot of people got into a lot of trouble over this one," he said—and he pulled from the envelope a navy-blue bound journal, gold-edged, about six inches by eight inches. A dark gold ribbon served as a page marker. He placed it neatly on the table. "This practically wrecked a playwright's life. And Kaufman in the thirties; he was the *king*. He was the golden boy. Everything he *touched* was a hit. He'd make a witty quip at the Algonquin on a Thursday night, and on Friday half the papers in the country were carrying it..."

*   *   *

Fifteen minutes later, Pannish pointed to Q.'s vest pocket. "You have to get rid of all pens—anything that might permanently damage the document. The shoulder bag, the pocket book, it's all got to go in the cabinet."

"I can keep a notebook, I hope?" said Q.

Pannish nodded, and he took a small cylinder full of half-sized pencils and put it on the table.

Then he took the pens and bags and locked them in a wooden closet with shelves. "Let me tell you a little story about Kaufman. I met him during the previews of *Once in a Lifetime*."

"We're a little tight on time," said Q. "But I would love to hear the story some time."

"Kaufman was just starting his collaboration with Moss Hart and..."

Pannish had moved down to the end of the table and sat in front of the computer, laboriously typing with one finger. "You know, Kaufman could only type with one finger, too. Did I tell you about..."

"Wow," whispered Sally. She ran her fingertips over the leather cover.

"In 1936, this was the Holy Grail," said Q. softly. "God knows how much the *News* paid for this. And how much damage it caused." He picked it up, weighed it in his hands. "This made headlines around the *world*. This tiny book. The New York playwright and the pretty little girl from Quincy, Illinois."

"May I?" asked Sally.

"Go ahead."

"Lavender ink!" said Sally. "I love it!"

In graceful feminine handwriting that looked like a meticulous schoolteacher's was written: *May 1934——*. The second date had never been filled in, but the last entry in the book was from Wednesday, September 9, 1936.

At the end of the table, with much commentary, Sid Pannish sat with a manilla envelope of clippings about the comedian Jonathan Winters, carefully summarizing the clippings into his computer. He had decided (so he explained laboriously) to start at the back of the alphabet, and had so far entered Z, Y, and X. It had taken him almost a year.

At the other end of the table, Sally and Q. were reading and transcribing entries.

Monday, June 17, 1935. Ah, desert night—with George's body plunging into mine, naked under the stars...

Friday, August 30, 1935. It's been years since I've felt up a man in public, but I just got carried away...

Sally said: "I can't believe this."

"It gets better," said Q.

Saturday, September 28, 1935. It was raining and lovely. It was wonderful to fuck the entire sweet afternoon away...

"They couldn't print those words in the papers in 1936, could they?" she asked.

"They probably skipped those parts."

"God, this makes me want to keep a diary," she said. "So if I ever want to read something really pornographic, I'll have it, like, close at hand."

"Always thinking ahead."

She stopped—ran her finger along the inner spine. "Somebody's been doing a little editing."

Q. squinted through his reading glasses.

She was right. A page from April of 1936 had been removed—you almost wouldn't notice, the tear had been made so precisely.

"Razored out," said Sally. "Like they do in the Dartmouth library."

In the previous entry, Ms. Astor had gone to San Francisco to visit friends. The page ended with: *It was pouring when we finally arrived at 891 Post Street, and D. was—*

"Who the hell is D.?" Q. asked.

"She talks about someone named Jose here. That's her friend. Maybe we can find out who he is, and then piece together who *his* friends are."

"The next page she's back in Los Angeles. Any further reference to D.?"

"Not that I've seen yet."

"If there's one thing I hate," said Q., "it's referring to a character by just an initial."

Sally turned to Pannish.

"Has anybody been in here to see the diary recently?"

"A handful of people a year come in. We had a guy from Bertelsmann who wanted to publish the entire thing, was going to make a facsimile edition right from her handwriting, but apparently the publication rights still belong to the Astor estate. Now Mary Astor died in— wait, wait." He moved his step ladder to the "A" cabinet and, with his back to them, looked at the notes written on the outside of a manilla folder. "September of 1987. But somebody in the family is hanging onto the rights."

"Has anybody been looking at it in, say, the last three months?"

"I believe so," said Pannish. "I can't tell you when exactly. Maybe a month ago? A middle-aged man— African-American—and a younger man—Caucasian. And then, I think, the younger man came back by himself the next day. He asked me to look up all sorts of things."

"Like what?" asked Q.

Pannish sighed. "About John Barrymore? Mary Astor apparently said John Barrymore was the love of her life, and he wanted a clipping on Barrymore. You know that Barrymore once sued the *News*? It was in the early 40's and—"

"What did he look like? The younger man?"

"You're asking an eighty-year-old man to remember? I take out my pills, I put them in my hand, and then, five seconds later, I can't remember if I just took them already. I walk into the kitchen, I say, 'All right, I know I came in here for something.' I think I'm suffering from C.R.S."

"What's C.R.S.?" asked Sally.

He thought a moment.

Scratched his head.

"You know, I have no idea... I think it was a joke."

CHAPTER TEN

NYPA

Friday. 1:28 p.m. When the body of Lilian Jackson Braun had been discovered in lower Manhattan, the New York Police Department had examined her cell phone records and contacted Q. He'd told them what he could—the mysterious "lavender ink." He'd never heard from them again until the previous day when Detective "Perca" Dan Davies from the 10th Street Station had asked for an interview. As Q. was already coming into the city for *The Daily News* appointment, he had agreed—and now he was sitting in John's Pizza on Bleeker Street, eating an entire pizza with fresh garlic—and a tankard of root beer—gormandizing his time away until his 3:30 appointment. Sally had gone home, and Q. looked at the delicious smelling, oily, garlicky, slightly-burnt meal before him and itemized everything that Stumpy Rabinowitz would find wrong with it: wheat allergy, dairy allergy, heart attack from the fat in the cheese, white flour turning instantly into sugar for diabetes, hydrogenated oils, cheese made with genetically-modified milk from bovine-growth-hormone-injected cows—and the root beer, my God, he might as well go directly to the oncology ward...

Considering all this, and carefully weighing his life expectancy against the smell of fresh roasted garlic, Q.

poured some oregano into his palm, crushed the leaves to release the flavor, sprinkled it judiciously on the pizza, and then wolfishly devoured the entire thing.

He wrote his own tombstone: *At Least He Fucking Enjoyed Himself.* "Turn your heads away, children. Mr. Qafka was a writer and, as such, a self-indulgent and depraved man. We can admire his work, but we can hate the man. Come along, children, let's move on to happier graves."

The humidity was evaporating before his eyes as he headed towards 237 West 10th Street. The sidewalk ginkgo trees, their leaves like pale green coins, fluttered in the breeze. A white cat watched him from an open second-floor window. One store sold nothing but exotic teas—its wooden walls painted dark blue, its floor filled with fragrant burlap bags; next door sold nothing but nuts—bins and bags and an old cast-iron peanut roaster that fragranced the air. What had O. Henry called New York: Baghdad on the Hudson? A nice phrase. Of course, the Baghdad image would have to be updated now to include Pastah El-Fahzoul's International House of Viruses (on 14th Street.) He imagined El-Fahzoul with his turban and his cell phone. "No, no, no—the coupon wrong. I know it say fifteen milli-liters monkey-pox, but it supposed to be *five* milliliters monkey pox. Hey, man, it's not my fault fuckin' *El Diaro* make a mistake. Yeah, well, fuck you, too, I hope you get Ebola, douche bag."

On the tile wall on 10th Street station was a large sign

of a police badge announcing: Greenwich Village Sixth Precinct. It was hard to read the sign because parked directly in front, right up on the sidewalk, was a mobile catering truck, and another truck whose insides were filled with cables and lights: a technician sat on the apron of the truck eating a sandwich, throwing the scraps to the pigeons.

Cables ran directly into the door of the station, which was braced open—and almost instantly a curly-haired cameraman in a teal tee-shirt, his eye jammed into a Sony Digital 1000 Betacam, was shooting into Q.'s face. On the side of the camera was stenciled a blue police badge with *NYPA* printed on it.

"Excuse me, but will you get that out of my face?" said Q. "I have no desire to be on your television show."

"We're doing a reality show," said a female voice over his shoulder, a production assistant: zebra-striped sundress, impenetrable sunglasses, long jet-black hair, earphones.

They were all walking together towards the front desk.

"I have no desire to be a part of your TV show, OK?" said Q. He held up a hand to the camera lens. "So turn that thing off. I very explicitly do *not* give you permission to use my image on the air."

"Keep rolling," said the production assistant. "Technically, sir, *NYPA* falls under the rubric of 'live news broadcast' so actually we don't need your permission, although we would like you to sign a waiver in terms of possible rebroadcast and editing."

"Film somebody else." Q. turned to the desk sergeant. "I have a 3:30 appointment with Detective Dan Davies. I'm James Qafka."

The production assistant came back immediately with: "James Qafka, the children's book writer?"

"I'm his twin brother, the plumber."

"Look," she said, "all we want you to do is act *exactly* like you normally would. We don't want the presence of the camera to be acknowledged or to influence you in any way."

"Down the hall," said the desk sergeant. "To the dark green file cabinet—and then left."

Q. moved in that direction; the cameraman and production assistant moving with him. He shook his head in disbelief at the stupidity of what was going on around him.

In the first aisle, another camera was shooting sideways. He glanced at what appeared to be the director, bearded and dressed in battle fatigues. "Don't look at the camera!" said the director, furiously shoving them along. "Just keep moving. Don't look at the camera!"

In the next cubicle he passed a girl, perhaps five years old, in an oversized pool robe, who sat staring down at the floor, the cameraman sitting in the chair next to her. Another director, in jeans, a ballcap, and an *NYPA* tee-shirt, sat on the floor.

The girl was near tears. "...and then he pulled me by the arm, and I cried out, 'Daddy!', and he pushed me into the car and—"

"Amy," said the director, and he held her hand. "This is beautiful, powerful stuff. But, sweetie, we just can't see your face. You're staring at the floor and all we've got is thirty seconds of your forehead. So what I want you to do is to tell us your story again, but this time I want you to cheat it a little bit. I want you to look at the water bottle on the chair, and I want you to pretend that you're telling the story to the water bottle. OK? Keep it rolling, Glenn. Buried Alive. Take Three. And, sweetie, don't be afraid to cry."

Detective "Perca" Dan Davies looked, to Q., to be in his mid-twenties. Everyone in power and authority, whom he had once looked up to, was now younger than he. It gave him no hope for the future. A generation not only stupid—but arrogant. As Harlan Ellison had pointed out, it was the worst possible combination: you couldn't argue or reason your way around it.

"Dan Davies, *NYPA*," he said, extending a hand.

"What the hell is *NYPA*?" asked Q.

The production assistant leaped in. "The initials NYPD are being claimed as the intellectual property of the New York Police Department, and, as such, would require a royalty. It's highly unlikely they'll win the case, but we're trying to cover all our bases."

"Now," said Davies in an overly-loud, overly-deep voice, "first of all, I want to take the trouble of thanking you for coming here today, Mr. Qafka. I know you're a famous and very busy man. But we're investigating the murder of Lilian Jackson Braun on August the eleventh, and Ms. Braun's cell phone records *appear* to—"

"Whoa!" said the sound man. "We're really popping the p's; I'm going to put a screen on it."

"One more thing," said the production assistant in the zebra-striped dress. "I don't want to insult our viewers, but I think, like, one in a thousand is actually going to know who Lilian Jackson Braun is. Can you give us the backstory? You know? America's most beloved blahblahblah? Tell us who she was. We've got to set this up better. Nobody's going to care if she's dead, if they didn't know who she was when she was alive. Can we possibly redo the whole bit where he comes in?"

"I don't see why not," said Davies. He straightened his tie in the mirror which was suddenly shoved in front of him. "Would you like some coffee?" he asked Q.

An intern instantly handed Q. a coffee mug with *NYPA* printed on it.

"You can keep the mug," whispered the intern.

As the PATH train moved into the long, sunny stretch after Jersey City, Q. stared at a photocopy that Davies had allowed him to keep. It was a handwritten attempt to trace the final hours of Lilian Jackson Braun's life—a slightly revised version of the list he had read earlier in the newspaper—a string of slightly disreputable gay, straight, S&M, and leather bars: The Azure Spheres, The Squealing Salami Lounge, The Smiling Altar Boy, El Lumpumpadero, The Pastoral Pipe Cleaner, and, finally, where she was found, poor thing, decapitated: The Bulgin' Marbles. In each place someone had identified her in the company of a young man—in his twenties or thirties—some thought he was bearded—others thought he was just swarthy. He was shorter than she was—that seemed to be consistent. One witness had him lip-synching to Chet Baker's recording of "Time After Time." The stories were inconsistent, but Lilian appeared to be a regular feature downtown. Everybody knew her.

Poon-Tang was biting his leg again. It was some sort of allergy, a hot spot, and Q. had picked up a packet of five milligram cortisone tablets (Prednisone) from the vet. He could barely read the tiny reading on the envelope: 1/2 tablet 2X daily for 5 days. Then 1/2 daily for 5 days. Then 1/2 every other day for TILL USED days.

He looked around the studio. Neither cat was to be seen.

They know, he thought.

He looked in the laundry basket.

He looked along the bookshelves and beams.

He found Ying-Tong on the windowsill behind the guest bed.

"Poon-Tang," he sang to the empty studio. "Poonie-Poonie-Poonie!"

He hoped the cat hadn't escaped. While Ying-Tong would remain inside even if the door stood wide open, Poon-Tang would be out in a flash.

He heard a male voice calling out, "Mr. Qafka!"

At the front door stood the Federal Express delivery guy.

"Sorry," Q. said. "I was looking for Poon-Tang."

"You, too?" said the driver.

*   *   *

Q. was sitting at his writing desk, transcribing his notes from the Mary Astor diary when melodramatic music suddenly blared forth from the television.

Poon-Tang reared back from the remote control, looking bewildered.

"Gotcha, my little friend," said Q—and scooped up the cat who offered no resistance. "And where have you been hiding, you little squirrel?"

He looked at the television as he found the remote control. An old black and white movie. The title card on the screen read: *Screen Play by JOHN HUSTON. Based upon the novel by DASHIELL HAMMETT.*

"At least you have good taste," said Q., and he turned off the set. He put Poon-Tang's collar on—a blue, jangly thing that Q. rarely attached except when catching the cat was vital. And he found the old lanyard cat-lead and clipped it to the unhappy cat.

In the kitchen, Q. carefully broke a cortisone tablet in half—and then, as sweetly as possible, forced it down the cat's throat.

Poon-Tang backed away—appeared to have successfully ingested the pill—and then spat it back out—perfect and undissolved.

Q. found an ancient crock of Wispride soft cheddar moldering away in the back of the refrigerator.

First, a smudge of unloaded cheese on his fingertip.

The sweet cat licked it gratefully away with its tiny rough tongue.

"Yes, I know you like a little cheese," said Q., in the time-honored tradition of speaking in syntactically-complicated English sentences to members of other species.

He offered another innocent, undoctored bit of cheddar.

Poon-Tang ate it with no suspicion or hesitation at all.

"And one *final piece* of delicious cheese," said Q.

He folded the half-pill into the cheese and offered it to Poon-Tang.

The cat sniffed it and swung his head away.

"Come on, now, you like this."

Poon-Tang lowered his head as far as he could, considering Q. had his neck in a choke-hold.

Q. forced the cat's tiny teeth open and physically put the doctored cheese as far down the cat's tongue as he could.

Q. let go of the collar to give the cat swallowing room—still holding onto the lanyard lead.

The cat swallowed and licked his lips.

"Thank Christ," said Q. "Such a good boy. Such a good boy swallows his pills."

At the sound of this offensive baby-talk, the cat promptly released the little pill back onto the floor.

All the cheese was gone.

The pill was untouched.

"God fucking damnit!" said Q. "There's no way I'm letting you go without this pill getting down your throat. I don't care if I'm here all night."

He reached for the refrigerator.

"OK, now, peanut butter. Kitty loves peanut butter. Mmmm... Organic peanut butter with no extra sugar added. Mmmm.. unblanched, organic Valencia peanuts—smooth style, just the way you like it."

He offered an unloaded fingertip of peanut butter.

Poon-Tang sniffed around it. Looked up beseechingly at Q., and then promptly devoured it.

"Excellent!" said Q. "And so good for my good boy. So healthy! And so untainted by hydrogenated oils."

He dipped his finger in again.

The cat ate it right up—licking laboriously.

"And one other tiny, tiny piece for my hungry kitty," said Q.

He tucked the pill into a pea of peanut butter and offered it exactly as he had the others.

The cat turned away.

"Oh, come on!" he said. "This is no different than the others."

The cat struggled valiantly—until Q. pried its mouth open—and inserted the loaded peanut-butter pellet.

Q. clamped his fingers around the cat's mouth—hoping the taste might convince him.

The cat stared at him in horror.

"Now you eat this," said Q. "You eat this for Daddy, and Daddy will open up sardines for you. Sardines. Mmmm..."

Poon-Tang pulled away.

The cat swallowed.

Q. scrutinized him carefully.

The cat drank.

No pill in the water.

Now the cat was exploring a paper grocery bag on the floor.

"Thanks God," said Q.

To celebrate, he washed a week's worth of dishes and glasses that were littering up the sink.

The late afternoon sun made the dishes miraculous vessels of light, water, and curved surfaces.

Q. stepped into the living room to enjoy the newspaper, when he heard the crunch underfoot.

He lifted his sandal.

The pill.

Half-crushed.

On the living room couch, Poon-Tang sat biting his back leg.

CHAPTER ELEVEN

NUMEROLOGY

Q. stood at the express check-out lane of the Kings in Garwood. He had only one item in his hand: sardines.

"Two-ninety," said the cashier—an astonishingly beautiful Hispanic girl. She held her arms like a dancer. Her name-tag read: Betsy.

Q. thought that if she worked in Los Angeles, she'd be in the movies. Here in New Jersey she was selling sardines.

He reached for his wallet—and there was nothing there

The other pocket.

Flat.

He cursed.

No change, no debit card, no credit card.

The girl said nothing, perhaps quietly enjoying his ineptitude.

I may be a pretty girl who's stuck working at Kings, her look said, *but at least I'm not some middle-aged fuck who can't even remember his own wallet.*

Behind him in line, an old couple was aggressively jostling him with their cart.

And he suddenly realized what had gone wrong.

He tapped his empty vest pocket for the third time.

Then he smiled.

Jesus, he thought, *I'm in Chapter Eleven.*

CHAPTER TWELVE

A REALLY BAD GIRL

Sallybikerun had sent him an e-mail saying that she had a lead on 891 Post Road in San Francisco, the address alluded to in Astor's diary. She wanted to run it down at the Rutgers library and would hopefully be in the office before noon. Q. liked that she called her desk the "office."

When he was in eighth grade he'd made a sign in Graphic Arts class that read—in giant block letters: *Bizarre Crimes Solved*. Thickly-inked blue letters on white cardboard. The only genuinely remarkable thing about the sign's extravagant claim was that he'd actually spelled "bizarre" correctly. He was in his Sherlock Holmes period then. He carried in his pocket, at all times, his black pocket magnifier and a tape-measure, just in case he had to calculate a suspect's height by the length of his stride.

What was appealingly prescient about the sign (which he had framed thirty years later and which hung now on the living room wall) was that, in a way, solving bizarre crimes was exactly what he did for a living. Most of the crimes were in the realm of his stories, but sometimes, as in the current investigation, they pressed in from the world around him. He looked at the yellowed sign: the dark letters of "bizarre" slightly crooked, and the "r" of "crimes" damaged on the lower serif—and he thought that, reproduced exactly as it was, it would make a good cover for a mystery book: strange and old and compellingly handmade.

He stood in front of the kitchen sink washing out the blender, listening to classical music on WQXR sandwiched between the endless commercials for Moskowitz Memorial Hospital with their fearful testimonials from patients who swore they would have been dead had not a "full body scan" caught their virulent illnesses. In his head, Q. imagined a more realistic testimonial:

WOMAN: When they told me Frank had Lampington's Disease I didn't know what to do. All I kept thinking about was Arielle, our four year old. How was I going to tell her? So I spoke to Dr. Moskowitz, and he said, "Look, your husband's going to be dead within six months—why do you want to spend all that money on him for? You're going to bankrupt yourself and your whole family." Well, thank God, I listened to Dr. Moskowitz because I withheld treatment, Frank died in two months, and now I'm living in a beautiful home in Short Hills with Dr. Moskowitz. And Arielle can afford that genuine sapphire birthstone bracelet she wanted so much. Thank you, Moskowitz Memorial Hospital. You saved my family."

Q. had been hearing this fantasy in his head while unscrewing the bottom of the blender, and he hadn't noticed that the warm soapy water was now funneling through the glass jar directly onto the front of his pants.

The doorbell rang.

Shit.

The front of his pants was soaked.

He thought about changing, but laughed instead, and moved to the screen door.

There, amid the screaming crickets, stood Hilary Olsen—sunglasses, in a one-piece cranberry dress.

"Did your toilet back up or are you just glad to see me?"

He smiled. She took off her sunglasses.

The Ivy-League rosebud, he thought.

"May I come in? I was passing by and I wanted to give you a present."

"A present?"

"Your birthday's next week, isn't it? Next Sunday?"

He figured she'd looked it up in *Something About the Author*.

She jostled a large black bag that said Bose Electronics on it.

Q. opened the door. He noticed the cranberry dress had no visible stitching on it—it clung to her body as if it had been custom made.

"It's not a Bose Radio," she said. "I mean, I like you, but four hundred and ninety-five dollars is too much for a guy I've just slept with once."

"Is that what the protocol says?"

"Absolutely." She flipped her hair behind her ear. "It's very clear about that. The only reason I even put it in this bag is because they paid for a product placement. But it's a *much* dandier present."

*   *   *

They sat in the kitchen. The coffee machine gurgled cozily.

Q. thought to himself: *OK, she's too crazy to sleep with again, but I'll be courteous.*

Yeah, right. And in the next scene she'll be sitting in the police station, with Newman staring at her no-under-wear...

"Is Sally here?" she asked.

This seemed to Q. an eerily intimate observation, but he answered truthfully: "She's down at Rutgers trying to solve a mystery."

"And what's that? Who killed Lilian Jackson Braun?"

"Sort of. It's what I mentioned to you before. Mary Astor's diary?"

"Really?"

"It's a very tangled web."

"Speaking of tangled webs," she said, and pulled back her hair again. "Are you going to open my present?"

"I'd thought I'd wait till my birthday."

"I don't believe in the future," she said. "Waiting. Everyone's always waiting. For what? Till the economy turns around? Till they're rushed off to the emergency room?"

"All right." He shrugged and lifted the wrapped box— about shoe-boxed size.

"Mahogany wrapping paper. Very masculine," she said.

"I feel my testosterone-levels rising already."

"In that case, I'll paper the whole house."

He tore the wrapping.

"This will definitely help you with tangled webs," she said.

It was a professional barber-type hair trimmer: black, metal-bladed, thick electrical cord.

"It'll let you go where no man has gone before," she said.

"No doubt," said Q. "Thank you very much."

"It's for your mustache, Mr. Panic," she said.

"I see."

"And any other hirsute object your writer's imagination might dream up."

He raised a hand. "I get it."

She added lightly: "Just an option down the road"—and she twisted her index finger in the air as if to say: *whatever*.

He poured coffee into her brittle, elegant cup; green tea into his.

"Tell me more about the case," she said. "I'm fascinated."

"Are you really?"

She nodded.

She really was an intelligent-looking woman, thought Q. Gwen's looks—but sharper, sadder, tougher. A husband who had no interest in fucking her, a condescending and self-adoring daughter. You sensed she was so angry she could light up a small city. Of course, it was exactly her rage that made the promise of sex so tantalizing—sex as a purely hostile act. But, no, he thought. He would be stronger than that. He didn't need any more insanity in his life.

He didn't have the strength anymore.

Resolved, he thought. We don't go to bed with her again.

He would show iron resolution.

"The death of Lilian Jackson Braun is, of course, being investigated formally by both the Westfield Police and the NYPD—or NYPA as we're now obligated to call them."

"I saw that show on TV," she said. "*NYPA*. It was touching. That little girl in the robe who talked about being buried alive. God, I couldn't breathe."

"I understand the water bottle she was talking to was deeply moved."

"What?"

"I'm involved in the case just as an interested observer. And because she telephoned me on the night she was killed."

"Right. You told me about the lavender ink and all that."

"Which I think refers to Astor's diary."

Hilary nodded.

"So the question then," said Q., "is why is this diary on her mind the night she's killed?"

"And why is she killed? Why is anybody killed? For money I would guess."

"Passion, too."

"Passion seems hardly the case here, does it?" she said. "I mean, I don't want to be rude, but this woman's, like, eighty, right? So are jealous octogenarians with chainsaws running around lower Manhattan?"

"The Wheelchair Killer!"

"My point exactly," said Hilary. "It hardly seems likely that some exile from Elderhostel is going to be running around Manhattan committing homicides. So the question is who profits by her death? Her books are worth a fortune, I guess. Who profits if she's gone?"

"Her husband. Earl Bettinger. A nice guy. I know him. Hated his wife, like every other husband I know, but no real motive to kill her."

"The money?"

"He gets the money now. Or at least half of it."

"Maybe he wanted it all."

"Why? She's a millionaire many times over—with the potential to keep generating more titles. It doesn't make any sense."

"Are there children?"

"Not that I know of. Plus you'd have to kill both parents if you wanted the money. No. Money seems to be out—and passion seems a little unlikely. But she was seen the night she died in the presence of a young man."

"How young?"

"Twenties. Thirties. Nobody paid that much attention."

"Well, I suppose passion might be involved there," said Hilary. "But it's a little weird."

No weirder than begging me to shave your pussy so you can pretend to be your daughter.

"There's a missing piece here, somewhere," said Q. "Ying-Tong, get away from there!" The silver Siamese was pawing at the electrical outlet on the countertop. "What the hell are you trying to do? Get away!"

Still the cat scraped away at the socket. Q. lifted her up and placed her on the sofa. "Now be a good girl."

"Me?"

"Well, you, too. But she's supposed to be the good one."

"That young man you said. Is there a name or a physical description?"

"Oh, you know the way it is—you talk to eye-witnesses, it's like talking to Ray Charles. He had a goatee; he didn't have a goatee. Nobody looks at anybody anymore. Particularly in New York. You look at a woman in New York for more than a half second it's the equivalent of saying: I want to rip your brassiere off with my teeth."

"That would be hard because I'm not wearing one."

"I wasn't speaking about you specifically."

"Too bad."

"I've never seen a dress quite like that. It looks as if it was knitted with you standing in it."

"It's called a body-dress—very trendy—no seams."

"It's pretty, Hilary. It really is. And if I were a younger man I'd act on my shabbier impulses. But I have a romantic commitment—one that's ten years old."

"You're dating a ten-year old? Well, let's hear it for open minds."

He poured her another coffee.

Resolve.

That's what he needed. Her revelation that she wasn't wearing a brassiere was beginning to stir his baser desires. (Specifically, his third-baser desires.)

"The passion theory has more angles," he said.

"Tell me."

"You said there might be a love interest—although that it seemed a little weird—still, she was seen in the presence, repeatedly, of this younger man. *One* of them might have been in love. But even more—she was a writer. What do writers do?" Q. wondered to himself why he was being so voluble and open with her, but at this point he couldn't seem to stop. Maybe it was that damn dress. "They *reveal* things. They use elements of real life, stories they've been told—and I think *that* might scare somebody."

"How so?"

"Aren't you the woman who said to me, please don't use this in one of your books?"

"Ah..." She bit her lip, adorably.

Resolve.

"Why? Because you were afraid that I'd reveal something that might embarrass you."

"*And* you. Lovable Children's Book Author Enjoys Ripping Off Married Woman's Brassiere With His—"

"You said you're not wearing a brassiere."

She held out her spoon like a microphone. "And how did you find out *that* particular piece of information, Mr. Qafka?"

"It would make a great scene for the English majors, wouldn't it?" he said. "*Qafka on Trial...* This joke'll work better on the audiobook."

"Here's one for your legal mind," she said, getting up and stretching her arms behind her head.

Her arms, he reluctantly noticed again, were in terrific shape.

"How about this?" she said. "A woman—let's say a relatively attractive, younger woman comes over here with the intention of enjoying some really unadulterated messing around."

"I don't like where this is heading."

"Hear me out, dude. So this younger woman, finding her amorous advances are, 'ow do you say in theese country—*rebuffed?*—decides to leave the gentleman's home, tear her four-hundred-dollar French seamless body-dress a little, just a little, drive over to the Westfield Police Station and tell them she was raped?"

He thought a second. The second was filled with *I'm fucked* repeated ten thousand times—alternating with *I'm so fucked.*

His face kept things light.

"And your evidence? Other than the tiny tear in your four-hundred-dollar French body-dress? By the way, do you appear brassiereless at the police station? Does that bolster your argument?"

"I might have left it here—being in such a hurry to leave."

"And where is it?"

"Anywhere," she said. "Why it might even be in that bag"—she pointed to the Bose Electronics bag across the room. "Along with my underwear."

The bag was out of his reach, and the interior of it was out of his sightline—any thought to get up and look would be to step deeper into the shit that was suddenly rising around him.

"If you tried to throw it out, that would even look worse," she said. "Not that I'd *do* any of this. Of course."

"And the physical evidence?"

"Do we really need that?" she asked. "Could've taken a shower—after I was defiled. You might not have ejaculated. And, of course, after we made love in the tub at my house the other day, whatever *did* happen to that towel?"

He wanted to kill her. (And after he'd killed her, he'd save the body-dress to try on later when he was alone.)

"Now I'm just saying those are things a really bad girl *could* do," she said. "A girl who got *rebuffed*."

"Right. But who'd want to have an affair with *that* kind of girl?"

"Exactly." She walked to the kitchen door and closed it. Locked it. "That kind of girl would be a drag."

Now she walked to the front—closed the wooden door and locked it. "But there's another kind of girl."

"Is there?" He walked into the living room. This time he was close enough to glance into the electronics bag.

It was empty.

"Oh, another kind of girl, and I think, another kind of guy. Much cooler. Both of them."

"I like this couple."

"A girl that'd never want to get her family involved in a scandal—or herself involved."

He nodded.

"A girl interested in something much more fun."

"My kind of girl."

"And the fact that you've got a ten-year commitment, and I've got an eighteen year one—I think that makes it sweeter. It establishes the ground-rules."

"And what exactly are the ground-rules? Bring your own towels?"

"No, it just means that if Polly's out of town and you feel like touching something soft, give me a call. That's all."

He was about to say, "I don't know—" but she put her finger on his lips.

"Let's not make any rules, OK?" she said. "Or plans? Or talk about the future? I told you I don't believe in the future. And if Harold and the kids are ever out of town, and I feel like touching something not so soft, I'll give *you* a call. All right?"

He was about to say something like: "I can't really sanction—" but she was stopping him again with a soft finger on his lips.

"What are you so scared of, Writer Man?"

CHAPTER THIRTEEN

COMMANDO-STYLE

That perfume again.

It poured off her shoulders—not sweet—but aching and overwhelming.

He pulled the cranberry-colored body dress off her. As she had suggested, she was wearing nothing beneath it.

"Commando-style," she said.

He looked down at this peaches-and-cream body in front of him, this gift, this barefoot, scented lady with her small delicious breasts and this area above her hips that felt as smooth as soapstone. Her firm, shameless stance. Her moon-face. Her armadillo tattoo. Her wide jade eyes—filled with the afternoon windowlight.

His hand followed the contour of her shoulder and breast and stomach.

"And your husband has no interest in this?"

"Don't call him my husband; call him Harold. The white girl's burden."

"Harold has no interest in this extraordinary prize?"

"Harold is scared of everything," she said. "Including me. He's scared of making a left-hand turn; he's scared of traffic; I think he's scared of his own sexuality."

He spiraled his right middle finger around her left

breast—drawing the circles smaller and smaller.

"What's he so afraid of?"

She looked right at him with her sun-lit green eyes. She exhaled before speaking. "I think he's afraid of losing control. And I told him, 'With sex, that's the point. You're supposed to lose control. And you trust the other person enough to do this kind of crazy trapeze act without a net—and after the madness, you both survive.' That's what he doesn't understand: the madness. These suspenders are ridiculous."

"They're the male equivalent of bra straps."

She looked at him with affection. "I'll miss you. When this is all over."

"I thought you said you didn't believe in tomorrow."

"I don't really. But I know the game." She undid his shirt and kissed his shoulder. "One day the guilt will get to you. You'll look in the mirror, at the circles under your eyes and say, 'What the hell am I doing?' And, a year later, you're driving up the turnpike thinking about some girl's naked ass standing in front of your bathroom mirror brushing her teeth and you think: 'What on earth was I thinking?'"

"You've got it all figured out."

"Right down to the naked ass," she said, and placed his hand on her firm rear-end.

"The honey-pot," he said.

"And it's all yours." And her words were lost in his mouth and her warm tongue was in his mouth and on his chin—a wet, *devouring* kiss.

"You're tense," she said.

"You could relieve the tension."

"Slow down, my baby, let's enjoy it."

"Let's cut to the madness."

"This is act one," she said. And she stepped back. "Let's take a bath together. Pull up all the blinds. And then we'll fuck our brains out. That's the second act."

"And what's the third act?"

"Surprise!"

She had the radio/CD playing classical music in the bathroom. Steam and perfume filled the air. It felt, to Q., as if time had slowed or stopped. She glistened. She looked younger with her hair wet, pulled back, pretty and androgynous. He closed his eyes to the classical music and the rhythmic dripping of the faucet. And for a second, the cats and the mysteries and the obligations were gone. Maybe she was right; maybe there was no tomorrow—only these sweet, sensuous seconds, drowning in an immediacy of sound and flesh and water and desire.

She was out of his old-fashioned clawfoot tub now—drying herself off before a steamed-up window. Now brushing her teeth. Erect and at ease. Her sun-tanned ass like a piece of fruit he wanted to bite.

The windowlight streamed in. She turned off the electric light, but the radio/CD went off, too, so she left it burning.

She disappeared for a moment and returned with a cardboard box.

It was the professional hair trimmer she'd brought.

Q., still in the tub, released a small, almost involuntary, sigh of disappointment. "I thought we could skip this part," he said.

"It'll be painless now," she said, "and I want to complete the fantasy."

She untied the black cord so it could extend to its full length.

"And what, exactly, is the fantasy?"

She buzzed the shaver once, like a race car driver testing his motor.

Then from her purse she removed what appeared to be a large, relatively realistic-looking rubber penis.

"This is new," he said.

"This is Bill," she explained. "My Boy Bill. Now we fill him up with warm water so he's ready for the fireworks."

She filled the warhead with water.

"The fireworks."

"Yes, the end of my fantasy."

She lathered a little soap on Bill and, leaning against the sink, used him to caress the opening of her vagina.

"Do you like this?"

"It's interesting."

"Is it getting you hard?"

"It's certainly keeping me awake."

She was working Bill more vigorously—penetrating deeper. "Say, 'I want to fuck you, Hilary. I want to fuck you until my balls ache.'"

"Do I have to?"

"It's part of the fantasy."

"I'd rather just admire you."

"Say, 'I want to fuck you Hilary. I want to explode inside your sweet cunt.' This is the fantasy." She didn't need him now. Her eyes were nearly closed and she was working hard.

"What's the fantasy?"

"To kill you and make myself come at the same time. Oh, sweet Jesus, fuck me, fuck me—"

With that she turned on the electric trimmer, and, while it was still buzzing, she tossed it towards the bathtub.

Horror went sweeping over him in a kind of terrible slow-motion—an electric charge of nausea rising up from his gorge.

He watched the electric trimmer arcing through the air.

He tried to haul himself up and out of the water.

He could hear her moaning against the sink—*fuck me, fuck me*—

A noise escaped his lips—some animal groan of *getmeout*—and he had one leg nearly out of the tub when he saw the razor about to hit the twenty gallons of water whose conductivity had probably been enriched with electrolytic bath salts—

—and there was a noise somewhere—

—and the light went out.

The radio/CD went dead.

The hair trimmer stopped buzzing as it hit the waterline and sank.

Both he and Hilary turned to the door.

Standing there, with her hand on the light switch, was Sally.

She held, in her other hand, Q.'s Newberry-Award-losing brass letter opener.

She fixed Hilary with a deadly serious gaze, and she spoke in the measured tones of a policeman trying to coax down a suicide jumper.

She said: "Put. The. Dildo. Down."

Then she spoke to Q. without taking her gaze from Hilary. "Sorry to interrupt, but it sounded like you might be in trouble."

Hilary suddenly lunged forward, and, holding Bill before her like a pistol, she squeezed a blast of water into Sally's eyes.

At the same time, she kicked a naked foot at Sally's legs.

Sally dropped the letter opener. She fell forward and smashed the toilet paper dispenser on her way down.

Q. was still standing with one foot in the water when Hilary went diving for the light switch. She slipped on the wet tiles, then regained her balance—and raised an arm towards the switch.

But Sally had grabbed the large black bathroom plunger, and she swatted it at Hilary's extended hand.

Hilary's right hand was diverted with the blow, but her left hand shot out for the light switch.

Q.'s left foot was rising from the water when the lights

went on again—and this time the tub buzzed and crackled with ozone.

The bathroom light was blinking wildly as, apparently, the circuit-breakers threatened to trip.

Sally and Hilary were facing each other—each slightly hunched in wrestling stance: Sally held the bathroom plunger before her—Hilary held Bill.

"En garde," said Sally.

A thrust.

A parry.

And they both went scrambling for the letter opener on the floor.

The light was flashing erratically; the radio playing in frantic spurts.

Q. didn't know what to do—naked, lumbering, dripping—but he had to do something.

He threw an orange plastic drinking cup at Hilary. Then he threw Polly's bottle of contact lens solution. *What the hell was there in a bathroom?*

He tried to grab Hilary. She was slippery in her nakedness.

Sally and Hilary were now wrestling on the floor.

The dildo spun across the tiles.

Q. grabbed it by the shaft and tried to beat Hilary in the head with the rubber testicles.

"The lights!" yelled Sally. "Turn off the lights!"

The two women were now on the rim of the tub.

Q. moved to the switch but slipped on the wet, soapy floor. His hand hit the wall as he went down hard.

The lights were still blinking and sparking—a frenzied classical march coming to life each second the power fired up the radio/CD player—recuing always to track one.

Q. grabbed a plastic razor blade to fight with—
Something.

He tried to kick Hilary, to punch her, slash her with a Bic disposable razor.

He looked around for something to club her with—

The Pepto-Bismol bottle?

The Milk of Magnesia bottle?

The melatonin tablets?

The electric toothbrush?

The catfight on the floor was out of control—someone smashed her head into the pipes below the sink.

Then Hilary grabbed his ankle and bit it.

Q. cried out in pain and tripped backwards towards the tub. He tore at the shower curtain—got a two-finger grip on it as he fell.

Pop. Pop. Pop.

The curtain rings pulled loose as his shoulder went down towards the electrified water.

The CD player re-cued to track one.

The second to last shower ring held.

No, it didn't.

Down he went.

He scrabbled for the recessed soapdish and managed, with every resource of strength he had, to keep his head an inch above the water.

"Sally!"

And just as Sally managed to knock the light switch down, his hand slipped, and his face plunged into the water.

Now Hilary was pushing his head down into the water, trying to drown him.

Sally pulled her off him.

Q. hauled his head up—the water streaming around him—he was coughing and gasping and choking.

Now the light was blinking again—that terrible electrical smell.

The CD player re-cued again to its frantic march.

Sally was an athlete, and instantly she spun around and faced Hilary, who had the brass letter opener in her hands.

"Fuck you!" Hilary yelled and came lunging towards Sally.

Hilary's foot landed directly on My Boy Bill which was lying in a soapy mess on the floor, and she went tripping backwards towards the tub.

Her feet spun. She threw out her hands to brace the fall—her ankles hit the base of the tub, and, screaming, she plunged backwards into the water.

The screaming.

And shaking.

For one terrible second her hands grabbed at the smooth tile wall.

The water bubbling and thrashing.

Then her hands gave way.

And her body fell limp into the electrified soapsuds, her legs still hanging outside the tub.

"I'm twenty years old, and I killed someone," said Sally.

"You didn't kill anybody."

"Oh, yeah, and how do you explain this one to the police? A naked lady with a twelve-inch dildo broke into your home and accidentally electrocuted herself with a men's hair-trimmer?"

"Just hold it."

"We have to call the police. Immediately."

"One minute, OK, Sally? *I'm* the one who was fucking the married woman here, all right? The prominent married woman with the high-profile attorney for a husband. That's all I need: Harold Duveen, Esquire, trying me for murder and the fornication of his wife."

"It wasn't murder; she was after *you*—she tried to kill you. The fact that she ended up killing herself was an accident."

"And how do I explain that?"

"Put a robe on, Q."

He slipped on his Egyptian broadcloth robe.

"Sally, I am *so* sorry to get you involved in this."

"I want to call the police."

"First, can we get our stories straight? The next five minutes are going to change both our lives. Let's handle it right."

Q. sat on the edge of the bed. Sally sat on a distant

chair. It was as if the act had been so horrific it physically kept them apart.

"Why did she come here?" Sally asked.

"I think she came over here to fuck me."

"OK, then why is she suddenly trying to kill you?"

"I don't know."

"Did she have some reason to hate you?"

"I don't know. I don't think so."

Sally was pacing around his bedroom now.

"And why the hair-trimmer?"

"You don't want to know."

"The police will want to know."

"We'll say it was mine."

"OK, and why is *she* using it?"

"All right. All right. You will never talk to me again, Sally, but she wanted me to shave her—I can't phrase this delicately."

"Go on."

"She wanted me to shave her pussy because she wanted to pretend she was her teenage daughter being fucked by her boyfriend."

A silence.

Sally looked at him with horror on her face.

"She wanted to pretend she was Gwen?"

"You know Gwen?"

"She was in tenth grade when I was a senior. We ran cross-country."

"Well, this was just an elaborate sexual fantasy. OK? It's something adults do. I'm not asking you to understand or be sympathetic."

"So she was Gwen—and who were you?"

Q. looked down at the floor. "I was Brad."

"You were Brad Lowry!" said Sally. "The lacrosse player!"

"OK. Laugh. Very funny. Very pathetic. Go tell all your friends at Dartmouth. I'm just telling you, this is an adult thing. You'll understand it when you're older."

Sally shook her head. "I'm just trying to imagine my mother asking some random guy to shave her pubic hair so she can pretend she's Sally. It makes me want to vomit."

"Fine. Vomit. And you want a *murder* trial roped around your neck? Gee, that'll put a little crimp into your New Hampshire social life this fall, won't it? Great. Go ahead and tell the truth."

"What's the alternative?"

"The alternative is that we *massage* the truth a little bit to save both our asses. The guilty have been punished. All the rest is window-dressing, all right? So we say that you and I were here working—*together,* OK—that's going to be important. Hilary Olsen shows up here because she's having air-conditioning problems at her house—"

"Is that even true?"

"She told me it was true." *The grease stain on her palm.* "And it doesn't have to be true. It's *her* trimmer. What she wanted to do with it is entirely her business. She goes to take a bath. And the next thing we know the lights are blinking, and she's accidentally electrocuted herself. We arrange her in the tub a little more in line with the story. And then we call the police."

"They'll never believe it."

"They *have* to believe it, Sally, because there're two of us. We corroborate each other's details. It may be improbable, but they'll have no other option *but* to believe it."

"I don't see why we have to lie."

"We have to lie because I can't explain why she wanted to kill me. And I don't want to find myself standing up in front of an inquest telling her husband that his wife asked some random guy she met in the grocery story to shave her—"

"All right, all right."

"And, look, before you find me so morally reprehensible—*you're* the one with the two boyfriends who don't know about each other, right? *You're* the one who, pardon the expression, is getting it from both ends?" Now Q. was pacing. Sally was sitting. "There's something here I don't get anyway. This woman is following me around—this is deeper than just some middle-aged stalking gig. I feel like I was set up, and I don't know why."

"You want to hear something weird?"

"I think I'm on Weird Overload."

"That tattoo on her shoulder."

"The armadillo?"

"Steve has the exact same tattoo."

"Steve at the bike shop?"

She nodded. "And think about what they told you in New York. Lilian Jackson Braun's companion on her gay-bar runs: short, goatee, lip-synching to Chet Baker's 'Time After Time.'"

"Yeah?"

"Steve sent me that song on a mix tape."

"Something is very wrong, Sally."

They sat for a moment together on the edge of the bed.

"We have to think this through."

"We seem to be sort of partners in this..." said Sally.

He nodded. "Let's clean her up and wait for the police to get here."

"We've got to clean up the bathroom a little; I ripped a fixture off the wall..." She closed her eyes. "I'll clean up the floor... Hide the dildo... Oh, and when I was at Rutgers this morning looking up 890 Post Road in San Francisco?"

"Right."

"In the 1930's Dashiell Hammett lived there."

"*The Maltese Falcon* Dashiell Hammett?"

She nodded.

"Whoa. We're opening something big here," he said. He looked at her. "Do you think you can handle this?"

"You always said I was 'dangerous.'"

CHAPTER FOURTEEN

PAPPY YOKUM

The ambulance had left with the sheeted body of Hilary Olsen.

The medical examiners had left with their flashbulbs and evidence bags and tape measures. (*To calculate a man's height from the length of his stride*, Q. thought. *Bizarre Crimes Solved.*)

Sally had left: silent, wary, nervous—My Boy Bill in her knapsack. "A souvenir," she'd said.

Harold Duveen, grieving husband, tearless in his three-piece suit, had been one of the last to leave. He'd spent most of the afternoon pacing around the front lawn talking into his cell phone—his courtroom voice so loud you could hear him from the living room. "I am *not* asking her first husband to the funeral," he was yelling. "I am *not*, is that clear? Number *one*—" and he was actually counting on his fingers on the front lawn: "The man has made my life miserable for eighteen years. OK? *Number two*—will you listen to me, Phyllis? You're my sister and I respect and love you, and you are *very* good at certain things. OK? If I wanted to return a coat to Nordstroms after I wore it for a year and a half and get a full refund, I would call you right up and say, 'Phyllis, I've got a job for you.' But there are also other areas at which *I* am good at—will you let me finish? Will you let me finish my point?"

And then one hour later he was out there again, speaking into his phone with even more solemn anguish: "Gwen, I told you to get your clothes off the fucking steps. I have asked for a *week*, OK? Now your mother's dead and people will be coming over to pay condolence calls, and I want the fucking clothes off the steps by the time I get home... No. No. No. Absolutely not. Gwen, consider it canceled. No further discussion. There is *no* way you're going to see the Dave Matthews band tonight. Not on the day your mother was killed. Hey, how you felt about her is irrelevant, OK? And I don't care how long you fucking waited in line for the tickets."

And then when talking to Detective Kingsley Ampersand and to Q., Duveen offered the fully-restored director's cut of *The Outraged Attorney*: "First of all—" the finger again—"I am *completely* unsatisfied with the explanation you've offered me about how my wife came to die, and if this is all you can offer, you can expect a complete *independent* examination of all the facts involved, and if you think Robert Shapiro had a field-day with Dennis Fung, wait till you see what Duveen, Hesperes, Heckyll, and Jekyll make of *this* half-assed bullshit; number two"—the finger— "every document in this examination, and I mean everything: every e-mail, every inter-office memo, every phone message will be subpoenaed by my office—will be *independently* corroborated..."

He finally spun towards Q. with the finger. "And as for

you, Mr. Qafka, I certainly hope your affairs are in order, and I don't use the word 'affairs' indiscriminately, because whatever your affairs are, the public is about to take a very long and uncompromising look at them." His cell phone was ringing now. "Good day, gentlemen. Normally I leave by saying you'll be hearing from my firm, but in this case you'll both be *living* with my firm for as far into the foreseeable future as you can possibly imagine." He handed both of them a card. And he was on the phone again as he got into his maroon PT Cruiser.

His exit might have been slightly more impressive had not the doors of his car been stenciled with yellow letters reading: *Been in an accident? Call 1-800-BIGSUIT*. Above it was a cartoon of a lawyer wearing an enormous zoot suit with money hanging out of all the pockets.

"Fuck all lawyers," said Ampersand, as the car pulled away. He was touching the back of his head, feeling around in his thinning hair.

"What do you keep touching your head for?"

"There's something there. I've been to four different doctors. They don't know shit."

"Let me look at you."

Ampersand bent down his head.

"It's a little fatty cyst, I know."

"Exactly. It's nothing."

"It's pink, right?"

"Yeah, it's perfect."

"Does it look any bigger since the last time you looked at it?"

"No. It's fine. Stop messing around with it. Go see a dermatologist if it bothers you."

"No, no, I hate doctors. But let me ask you something."

"All right."

He moved a little closer on the front step. "That girl who was here with you?"

"Sally. She's my assistant. She's only here during the summer. And on holidays."

"Yeah, yeah. Let me ask you one thing: Are you fucking her?"

"Oh, come on, Ampersand. She's twenty years old. She's my assistant; I'm not jeopardizing that."

"OK, OK," he said, raising his hands in defense. "Does she have a boyfriend?"

"What are you talking about?"

"I think she's hot."

"Oh, yeah, she really wants to date a fifty-five year old fat fuck with a fatty cyst on his head."

"Look at Duveen and his secretary."

"He's a rich and powerful attorney, for Christ's sake. It's like dating Tony Soprano. Women *like* that. Look at you. It's like dating Pappy Yokum. Give me a break. And stop touching your head for Christ's sake."

"It feels like there's something there. Like my skull has lumps on it. Like something's growing. Like I have brain swelling or something."

"So go see a doctor."

"Forget it. Those sons of bitches'll kill you."

*   *   *

Sally called Q. about an hour later.

"Can we talk on the phone?" she said in a voice that was barely audible.

"I don't know whether they listen in on phone conversations or whether that just happens in books," said Q. "At any rate, I don't think Ampersand is listening in; he's too busy feeling his skull for brain swelling."

"It's not the police I'm worried about..."

Q. stared out the window. "OK," he said—thinking of a place no one could identify by name. "Can you meet me at seven at the Love Shack?"

"I don't know where you mean," she said.

"Remember you showed me that place where kids used to fool around?"

"I honestly don't remember."

"In the woods."

"What woods?"

"Tamaques Park."

"I'm not trying to be difficult, I just don't—"

"By the abandoned rifle range."

"Q., I'm just not with you on this."

"You know, off Lambert's Mill Road, I told you we used to go and collect rifle shells there when I was a kid?"

"You told me this?"

"And when I was in elementary school I lost the silencer to my Multi-Pistol 09—this toy where the pieces fit into a little plastic attaché case? And I told you for the next twenty years, whenever I walked around there, I still looked for it?"

"Are you sure this wasn't someone else?"

"And there's this little cinderblock frame there—falling apart now, and somebody had sprayed *Love Shack* on the side in silver paint, and you said that couples from the high school went there when they were looking for a place to have a secret rendezvous? Come *on*, Sally." Q.'s voice was rising in irritation.

"Wow. I'm drawing a complete blank on this one."

"Well, that's the place where I want to have the secret meeting."

"You better give me the directions again."

"Forget it. Let's meet at the Big Rock."

"The Big Rock?"

"Down by where I used to live?"

"I'm not with you here, Q."

"Jesus, *you* name a secret place."

"All right," said Sally. "You remember that *outdoor* place told you I had sex with Steve and Eddie on the same day, just two hours apart?"

"What if Steve is listening? He'll know the spot."

"He doesn't know I met Eddie there."

"Yeah, well how many *outdoor* places have you had sex with Steve at? It can't be that hard to figure out."

"How many outdoor places? I would say at least thirty."

"Jesus Christ, Sally, you've got to clean up your act."

"I told you; it wasn't romantic for me. And the problem wasn't me. It was Steve. He always wanted to get his rocks off."

"Steve, if you're listening, you are one sick fuck."

"Well, at least he never brought over an electric shaver."

"Hey, *I* didn't bring that. *She* did."

"The Big Rock," said Sally.

"What?"

"I just remembered where that is."

CHAPTER FIFTEEN

LOW-ABILITY CAT

"Steve called me up right after you did," said Sally. "He wants to go out tonight."

"You're crazy if you meet with him alone."

"How can you call this the 'Big Rock'?"

"When I was little it was big."

They stood on the corner of Rahway Avenue and Norwood Drive—a block from where Q. had been raised.

"I mean, people put stones like this in their gardens."

"OK, so I'm five years old: what am I supposed to say? 'Meet me by the relatively medium-sized rock?'"

"I would have said, "'Meet me at the corner.'"

"Well, that's why they accepted you at Dartmouth. Let's walk."

"You nervous?"

"I think your friend Steve is mentally unbalanced enough that I want to keep moving."

Like some slightly bizarre couple, they walked slowly around the semi-circle that was Tamaques Way.

"When I was little I called this street—"

"Let me guess: The Big Circle."

"Smartass."

"Am I right?"

"Of course you're right. Dartmouth. Early decision."

"I wish I knew what that tattoo was all about. That's the really scary thing. When I saw her lying there in the tub—with *that* on her shoulder. That scared me."

"Did you ever ask Steve about it?"

"Yeah. He said it was a fraternity thing."

Q. stopped.

"That's basically what she said to me."

"They've obviously agreed on their story. Of course, it could actually be a fraternity thing."

"Did he ever mention Hilary Olsen?" asked Q.

"No. Of course, he's probably fucked every woman in Union County. I think he got a printout from the Voting Board, and he's working down the list like some tireless little—I don't know—what's the word for guy ho-bag?"

"...Male bag?"

"I mean the name for some totally amoral, skank-ass, saliva-dripping poon-rat."

"I think the term is: Member of Congress. Can I ask you something?"

"Why am I dating him?" said Sally. "I know, I know."

Q. shrugged.

"You know what my roommate says? She says it's because I basically hate myself. And that I want to rub my nose in shit."

"That's a heavy judgment to pass down on a friend."

Sally offered no reaction to this, and Q. let it pass.

He looked at the older, dowdier houses and said: "When I was young, I used to ride my bike around this cir-cle and pretend that I had built the whole block as a fantastically detailed movie set—every home, every interior, the kid's toys littered on the front lawns, the sprinklers running. It was the greatest set that anyone had ever constructed." He pointed dramatically. "...And I think now, sometimes, since all my stories have been set here, that I actually *did* construct a vast film set, and that I'm still playing with it."

"I'm afraid to go home," said Sally. "I think Steve'll be waiting for me at my folk's house."

"We could go to the police."

"And say what: I'm scared of a tattoo?"

"Ask them to follow up the lead that Steve was the guy with Lilian Jackson Braun the night she was killed?" said Q.

"The lead? What possible grounds do we have to say that?"

"You could testify that's he's a totally amoral, skank-ass, saliva-dripping, what was that word?"

"Poon-rat," said Sally.

"Well, at least it would be the first time the word 'poon-rat' ever appeared in a police report. I've got an idea," said Q. "The library is open till nine; let's go there to find out what we can about Dashiell Hammett. And then you spend the night at some friend's and—"

"And where are you spending the night?"

"I was planning on walking back home."

"And you feel safe there? Everybody knows where you live. You're, like, the town celebrity. If this woman was willing to kill you—and she's part of some sort of organization—if that's what the tattoo means—you don't think somebody else would try the same thing?"

"That's reassuring."

"Think it through," said Sally. "Do you really think she was willing to murder you just because you wouldn't shave her pu—"

"Drop it, shall we?"

"What I mean, Q., is that she was willing to kill you because you were onto something. *We* were onto something." Sally was serious now—and sounded legitimately frightened. "And what's changed? Nothing except she failed at what she set out to do. So what happens now? You're the head of some sort of secret organization and your first agent fails; what do you do?"

"You send another."

On the second floor of the Westfield Public Library, most of the patrons had already left—the library would only be open another fifteen minutes, a female voice had announced.

But Sally was fast. She clicked and scrolled through what was once affectionately called a card catalogue.

She cross-checked information with the small notebook she kept in her backpack.

"We know Hammett was living at 890 Post Road in the late twenties—so let's assume he was still there in the mid-thirties when Mary Astor came to visit."

"That was the missing page in the journal, correct?" said Q. "I mention this for the benefit of readers who

might just be skipping around looking for the pornographic parts."

"There's no reference to her visit in any Hammett letters I've been able to find. But you figure it out. Why
would she be visiting Dashiell Hammett in San Francisco
in April of 1936? John Huston doesn't make *The Maltese
Falcon* until 1941."

"Huston's out in Hollywood. He may be negotiating for
the rights," said Q. "He might be using Astor's good looks
as a calling card—even as a signing bonus. I don't want to
be crass about it, but Mary Astor was no sexual shrinking
violet—if she saw the opportunity for a magnificent star-
ring role—and saw that sleeping with Hammett or Huston
would get her the part, I don't think she'd hesitate."

"The time lag bothers me," said Sally.

The library will be closing in ten minutes.

"Even if they signed her," said Q., "how could they film
the story at that time? With an actress involved in the
hottest sex scandal since Fatty Arbuckle? They had to let
it cool off a few years."

"Who's Fatty Arbuckle?"

Q. sighed. "Don't they teach you anything at college?
He was an early rap-star. He and Biggie Smalls did a lot of
work together. Fatty and Biggie they called themselves."

"The problem is that Hammett is not keeping a journal."

"When did he write *The Maltese Falcon*?" said Q.

Sally knew the answer without looking up from her
work. "1929. I've got a copy in my backpack."

Q. flipped through it. "*Dedicated to Jose.* Who was

Jose? His landscaper?"

"Jose was a woman, believe it or not, Mr. Enlightened Multi-Cultural Author," said Sally. "It's complicated. Wait a minute." She turned to Q. "OK. Hammett publishes *The Maltese Falcon* in 1929—so he's writing it, what, the year before?"

"Or earlier."

"So we go back to when he's writing it and find out what's on his mind then."

The library will be closing in five minutes.

The lights began going out.

"I don't follow," said Q.

Sally was talking fast now. Her eyes were lit up. "Astor and Huston come over to talk about the book and the movie. Somebody considers what they talk about so dangerous or—I don't know—so *incriminating* that they razor the page right out of Astor's diary. And apparently the information is so dangerous that Lilian Jackson Braun might have been killed to protect it."

"Possibly."

"Possibly. So, OK? What do they ask a writer? What's the question most people ask you about your books?"

"How much money did you make?"

"OK, what's the next question."

"The next question is: 'You know, I've got an idea for a novel myself, sort of my life story, but I don't know where to begin. Could you possibly write the whole thing for me—and then let me complain about every single sentence that you write?'"

"I'm talking about *polite* people. What do polite people ask you?"

"They say: 'Can you get me a copy? I'd love to read it.' Notice the wording there. Not can I *buy* a copy; not can I order a copy—but can you *get* me a copy? In other words, 'I'm fascinated by your work, fascinated by you personally, James, but if I have to spend one fucking penny on it, forget it.'"

"Come on, I've been to book signings; what is every author asked?"

They spoke it together:

"Where do you get your ideas from?"

"So get this," said Sally. "Get this. I am getting excited about this."

The computer clicked off. It was nine p.m.

"Fuck. I'll finish my research at Jillian's. But *listen*."

"I am."

"They ask Hammett where did you get the idea for *The Maltese Falcon* and he tells them about—"

Q. finished her sentence. Her enthusiasm was catching. "—*a real life legend*. The book is based on a real object. Something that really exists. My God."

"OK, the *novel* is about a made-up falcon encrusted with jewels—but the story is *based on something real*."

"So these guys trying to kill us are modern treasure hunters," said Q. "Chasing after some legendary artifact! Something to do with the tattoo. And they're afraid we're on to them! Jesus, what a yarn! This is gonna put Shakespeare back with the shipping news! As Preston

Sturges once said."

"Who's Preston Sturges?" said Sally.

Q. returned home briefly and deliberately left the lights off. As he checked his phone messages, Ying-Tong jumped on the couch and climbed on his shoulder. The last time he had seen her she'd been pawing an electrical socket in the kitchen—how prescient that now seemed—and for a terrible moment he saw, again, Hilary Olsen falling backward down into the bathtub—her hands extended to slow her fall, the same hands which a half-second later would conduct enough voltage to stop her heart.

The cats seemed to know everything.

Maybe animals really were divine spirits—vessels of God which served as conduits to a half-blind mankind...

"Yow!" cried Poon-Tang from the rafters above.

"I know you're hungry, poor kitty." He took out a tea saucer. "And Daddy's got your favorite: corned beef. Mmmm." From the refrigerator he unrolled some tinfoil with remnants of his sandwich from Deli-King. He broke it into little pieces over the saucer. Poon-Tang was right beside him on the counter, licking his tiny lips—his poor back paw looking like a red stump where he'd been biting and licking it incessantly. "Yes. Delicious corned beef. The *juicy* not the lean. Now just one minute."

He took from the window ledge the white envelope from the vet's—shook out a half-tablet of cortisone, and carefully hid it among the shards of corned beef.

"Your favorite!" said Q., and placed it on the floor next to the water bowl. "Now eat it all up. Good kitty!"

It took less than thirty seconds for Poon-Tang to consume the entire saucer of meat.

Q. put on his glasses.

No sign of the pill.

"Good boy. Such a good boy eats his pill."

The cat looked up agreeably. Licked his chops once. On the bridge of his nose was the untouched pill—perched there like a tiny sugar cube.

"How can you *do* that?" Q. cried. He reached to grab him, but the cat was gone—up the steps towards the books on the second floor. "You little ungrateful monster! After all I've done for you, you can't eat one fucking pill. Come on, Poonie, give me a break!"

Q. slumped back on the couch.

Ying-Tong had knocked a stack of his sheet music off the piano and onto the floor, and she was lying indolently on top of "Melancholy Serenade." She yawned, looked up at Q., and turned her head to the side as if to say: "Poon-Tang is a burden we both have to bear. It's difficult, but we've got to be patient and forgiving. He's a low-ability cat."

Then Q. called up Philip Roth and asked to meet him at White Rose.

"You're suddenly dying for a cheeseburger at two in the morning?" said Roth.

"I'm buying," said Q.

"I'm there."

CHAPTER SIXTEEN

LODGE BROTHERS

"May I say something that sounds egotistical?" said Roth. "This is something I can only say to you, and you can't repeat it, but, honestly, every single one of my books should have been given the Pulitzer Prize. Every single one of them. From *Goodbye, Columbus* on. Now I know that people would hear that and say, 'My God, that man is an egomaniac; no one could be that full of himself.' But I'm sitting here telling you the truth, Q. Every one of those books was the funniest, smartest, and cleverest piece of work that came out in any given year. Am I right? Five major works in the 1990's. Did you know that? And I swear to God every single one of them should have gotten the Pulitzer. You put this in your book, I'll kill you, but would you tell me, also, why I haven't gotten the Nobel Prize yet? Fucking Saul Bellow got it in '76, that libidinous no-talent fuck, that great patriarch of the Jewish-American novel, let's all fall at his feet and kiss his golden matzoh balls! You know what he prints on his dust jackets: *He is the only novelist to receive three National Book Awards.* Jesus H. Christ, can you imagine somebody so full of himself. And may I mention, I've won two National Book Awards, plus the National Book Critics Circle Award—which I know is like Miss Congeniality, but it's still a national award. Oh, that jealous son of a bitch, he's probably sitting in Chicago sweating every night that I'm going to win a third one and knock that sentence right off every fucking book-jacket he'll ever print. He's probably on the phone right now, calling Charles McGrath at the *Times Book Review*, 'Did you read the new Philip Roth, Chuck? God, it fucking *sucked*. Oh, you've got to *slaughter* it.'"

"Not too bitter, are we?"

"I am not bitter," said Roth. "I am genuinely not."

He held his hands out as if to say: not guilty.

In the middle of a dark and shuttered Highland Park, White Rose was lit up like an operating room. Roth and Q. sat at their usual window seat. In the white fluorescent light Roth looked even more cadaverous than the last time he'd seen him: washed out, grim, in that same terrible green military jacket. Q. thought he looked like a man who had false teeth but who refused to wear them: something shrunken and frowning about the mouth.

"Lighten up," said Q.

"That's good advice."

"It's three in the morning, what are you so pissed off about? You know what you look like—what Harold Duveen said about his first wife—like you're perpetually smelling shit."

"I am perpetually smelling shit," said Roth. "And it's called America."

"Just keep telling that to the Nobel Prize committee."

"They hate America, too. Or certainly white America. Particularly old-school Jewish White America. Do you think I wouldn't have gotten the Nobel yet if my name had been Mubutu Zamboni Exclamation Point? I would've won *six* of them! Plus I'd be head of Black Studies at Harvard."

"Eat your fucking hamburger, Philip."

"What the hell do we eat these for? *Trayfe drek*, as they say at the Black Studies Department at Harvard."

Roth was playing "Rockin' Around the Christmas Tree" on the jukebox for the third consecutive time.

"Look. Philip. I need to talk to you about that woman who died in my house. I got some new developments."

He did his elderly-Jewish-man-in-Florida voice: "Believe me, it vassa *blessing!* The best *thing* ever could have happened. She vants you to shave her twat? I never *heard* from such a thing. What kind of *behavior* is that from a civilized person? Feh, you're lucky she's gone." He began coughing, and at first Q. thought it was part of the impersonation—but it went on too long.

Q. slapped his back.

"What the fuck are you doing?" said Roth.

"I'm trying to help you."

"Sixteen years, the chiropractor has finally got my lumbar adjusted, and two good *hocks* from you and it's right back where it was. For this I should be thankful?"

"Can I stay at your place tonight, Philip?"

He stopped and stared. "You really are afraid."

"I don't know what's happening anymore. There's some kind of, I don't know, conspiracy. Somebody's scared I've stumbled onto something. They're willing to kill me for it. And the strangest thing is, for the life of me, I'm not sure what it is."

Roth rubbed the knuckles of his index finger over his five-o'clock shadow. "Well, you're more than welcome to stay with me. Although I hate to think you're actually in trouble. Of course, they've got me staying in a shithouse. That's Rutgers for you. Some frathouse that lost its license. Ancient orange carpeting and a filthy toaster oven: the smell of sloth and debauchery in the stairwells. You'll probably love it." He coughed again, messily, and spat some vile-looking mucus into a napkin.

"You really should see a doctor," Q. said.

"You think I haven't seen a doctor? You ever hear of Doctor David Hoffmann, the pulmonary specialist at the Hospital for Special Surgery? The author of *Change Your Breath; Change Your Life*?"

"Yes."

"Me, too. I wonder what he's doing tonight?" He coughed again. "I wonder if he's eating a cheeseburger? *Trayfe drek.*"

"Are you going to be all right?" Q. asked.

"I'm going to die," said Roth. "And you want to hear a secret: You're going to die, too. And *he's* going to die." He pointed to the counterman. "And everybody else in this restaurant, every single one of them—so full of piss and vinegar. All of them will die. That's what we do. We drink coffee. We check out women's tits. We jerk off. And they bury us in a box wearing a tallis we haven't looked at since we were thirteen. Oy, it takes the *wind* out of everything, doesn't it?" He squinted at the cars passing outside. "Did you ever think what you'd do if you knew you only had a few weeks to live? I remember seeing that interview with Dennis Potter, the television writer, a few months before he died from pancreatic cancer—he knew he was going to die—it was histologically unstoppable—and he said that he'd contemplated going out and killing Rupert Murdoch."

"Why Murdoch?"

"It was political for him. Murdoch represented everything he hated: the trashing of British culture, the stupidification of the press, of publishing, of television. And Potter actually thought about doing it." Roth belched and fanned away the fumes. "I felt that right in my pancreas."

"So why didn't Potter do it?"

"Oh, his work, of course. Writers are whores to their work, to their insufferable vanity. If they could write one more paragraph on the lids of their coffins they'd do it." He whispered like the last croak of a dying man: "'Kid, send this lid to the *Times*, will you? It might make a good last page for the magazine section.' But tell me more about this conspiracy of yours. Jews are always looking for conspiracies, aren't they? Jews never want to say people hate us because we're loud, complaining, and totally self-absorbed—no, they hate us because we wear mezuzahs." He did the burlesque musical-tag from *Laugh-In*: "Yah-dah-daht-dadot-daht: mezuzah!" He delivered the last word in the vintage Arte Johnson dirty-old-man voice.

"You're still watching *Laugh-In*?"

"It's like something from the moon," said Roth. "Leering middle-aged men making boob jokes about Sophia Loren and Racquel Welch. You can't imagine that it ever existed! A whole country in love with the catchphrases! 'We've got to stop meeting like this; I think Harold is getting suspicious!'"

The phrase jogged Q's memory—and he took a napkin and drew with his pen what looked like the armadillo tattoo he'd seen on Hilary Olsen. He placed it in front of Roth. "Does this look familiar to you?"

Roth said: "You know something, it actually does." He put a finger to his forehead. "I have a book back in Connecticut; maybe the Rutgers library has it, I used it for *The Human Stain*—something about a history of Masonic Lodges or fraternal organizations or some such bullshit, but I'm pretty sure this is on the cover. I can't think of any other way that I'd remember seeing this. It's an old book, maybe the '20s? Something, something, *Masonic Mysteries*? A history of secret fraternal societies? I'm getting it wrong, but I have it at home. I found it in some used bookstore. The *books* were new, but the *store* was used! Haha!" He drummed his hands on the counter. "Yah-dah-daht-dadot-daht: walnetto!"

CHAPTER SEVENTEEN

LIKE WEBSTER'S DICTIONARY WE'RE MOROCCO BOUND

Sallybikerun and Q. were running to catch the PATH train to Manhattan. They had rendezvoused at the Newark station. It was 11:09 in the morning. They made it into a car that was nearly full. Some Caribbean musicians were playing for tips (steel drum, a horn player who played two trumpets simultaneously, and an upright bass.)

"Good music," said Sally.

"We're back in business!" said Q.

"Please, not again!"

And, quite astonishingly, they both sang to the melody of "The Road to Morocco," as the Caribbean combo played the jaunty accompaniment.

BOTH: We're off on the PATH to Manhattan!
SALLY: Just, please, promise me, no more songs.
Q: I must admit these melodies
         Don't make a lot of sense.
SALLY: They forfeit your credulity
         And trash all your suspense.
Q: They're best if you turn down the sound.
BOTH: Like *Webster's Dictionary*, we're Manhat—

"The pun doesn't quite work anymore, does it?" said Q.

"Not exactly," said Sally.

At the 42nd Street library, Sally sat at one of the old microfilm readers—the reels whirling and rewinding with a frightening racket. Q. sat next to her, impressed with her speed, focus, and technical proficiency.

"I found the original book review," said Sally, "in *Proceedings, the Journal of the Society for Psychical Research*. Look at this. *Masonic Mysteries: The Book of Forbidden Knowledge. Emblem, Talismans, and Charms Revealed! Being a History of Fraternal Secret Organizations.* This had to be what Roth was talking about. *By Paul Heuzé. Les Editions de France. Translated by Harry Price and Eric Dingwall.*"

"The year?"

"1928. Dashiell Hammett could definitely have seen this book," said Sally. "I'm just hoping there's a graphic."

The reproduction was poor. She flipped to a more powerful lens—which only magnified the imperfections in the film.

She turned the crank and framer—and adjusted the viewing head.

A smudgy square about the size of a matchbox came into view. It was hard to make out on the screen: a pen and ink drawing of a sort of court jester pulling aside the curtain of a dark cabinet. Floating in the darkness of the cabinet were a smiling skull and numerous other mystical and astrological signs.

"Give me a quarter," said Sally.

She printed the page—which disappeared from the screen for about five full seconds—and then a wet copy, smelling of chemicals, came coiling out the side of the machine. The image was printed as a negative—so now black symbols floated in a white cabinet.

"The perfect time," said Q., "to take out my Bausch and Lomb, ten power, Coddington pocket magnifier that I bought when I was twelve years old from the Edmund Scientific Company formerly of Barrington, New Jersey, and which I have been carrying around in my pocket ever since." He removed the magnifier from his pocket, swiveled open the thick black lens from the aluminum sheath—the lens was as thick as his thumb—and he bent down lower over the printout.

"Impressive," said Sally.

"Bizarre Crimes Solved. A lot of this looks like Tarot stuff: queen of wands, pentacles."

"What's that?" asked Sally. She pointed at something printed on the curtain the figure in motley was drawing aside.

Q. lowered his head closer to the page.

What came into focus was the terrible face of the jester—wearing a mask that made him look like an insect.

Q. lowered the lens to the folds of the curtain: a half moon, a star, and there near the bottom, distorted in a magnified microfilm from a magazine published nearly eighty years earlier—was the figure of the armadillo.

Sally took the lens and studied the figure.

Neither one said anything.

"Ms. Corcoran?"

The voice came from the ancient and elongated librarian who looked, himself, as if he might have belonged to the Society for Psychical Research in 1928.

"Our catalogue shows we have the volume you requested. *Masonic Mysteries*. And it's not checked out. But..." He shrugged. "It appears to be missing."

The Bulgin' Marbles, a walk-down club on Barrow Street, may have looked alluring and fraught with lascivious possibilities at night, but in the torrid sunlight of two p.m. it only looked tired, neglected, and slightly squalid. The bar was open—but empty—when Q. and Sally took the three steps down to enter the place—which smelled of urine, disinfectant, and cigarettes.

A ceiling fan turned.

Chet Baker sang "Time After Time" on the CD player.

Sally touched his arm. "The song Steve put on the mix tape." She looked around. "I can't believe this is where she died. I wonder if her ghost is still around."

"If I were a ghost, I wouldn't hang around someplace that smelled like somebody just took a piss on the floor."

There was a large framed print on the wall of a statue of a nude woman kneeling on a pedestal of stone, her right arm coyly touching her toe, while a nude man adoringly buried his face against her left breast, his hands also behind him.

Sally seemed mesmerized by it. "What's that up his

ass?" she whispered.

"That's the stone he's kneeling on."

"Oh, yeah?" She rolled her eyes. "I think he's more interested in the stone than in her breasts."

"This is a famous sculpture, Sally. By Rodin, I think."

"I saw that movie," she said. "The giant flying dinosaur."

"That's *Rodan*. He did very little sculpting."

A quiet male voice came from the dark restaurant.

"Can I help you? I'm Tom."

From the shadows came a strong-looking man, perhaps in his mid-thirties, dressed in a black tee-shirt and black jeans—no socks or shoes. He looked, in this dark place, incongruously sunburned, as if he might have just stepped off of the beach. Extremely short black hair; cratered skin that suggested he might have survived once-terrible acne. His ears were strangely pointed, like an animal's.

"You definitely look like two lost souls," he said—the voice gentle, humorous, so soft it was difficult to hear.

"I was just admiring your art," said Sally.

"*L'Eternelle Idole*," said Tom. "I love the shape of her breasts. 'Majestic moons,' Michael Cunningham used to say. Michael used to come here a lot before he won the Pulitzer Prize. Now, alas, his taste is a little more *recherché*."

"Do you know this guy?" asked Sally, and she handed him a photograph.

Tom examined the picture.

"Nice car."

"Yes, and do you know the guy?"

"My dear, we all know Steve."

Sally was stunned into twelve seconds of silence.

Q. spoke: "He was a regular here?"

"And everywhere else. Steve is rather legendary downtown. 'Stallion Steve'? 'The Studhorse of Sheridan Square'?"

Sally was turning pale. She looked away.

"Did you ever see him in the company of this woman?" Q. handed him the book jacket photo of Lilian Jackson Braun.

Tom turned away in melodramatic revulsion. "Please, God, I never want to see that woman's face again. Is *that* what this is about? Please! I've talked to the police; I've talked to the reporters; I have nothing more to—"

"No, we're friends of Steve's," said Q., flying blind now. "We haven't seen him for two days. He hasn't been home and—"

"You're his family?"

"No, just friends."

"Well, then I can't really imagine you'd be worried if you haven't heard from Steve for a few days, or if he hasn't been home. I didn't even know he *had* a home."

"But you'd seen the two of them together?"

"Absolutely. But she was *always* surrounded by people."

"She came here often."

"Two or three nights a week. I never liked her. Carl, the bartender, he adored her. Thought she was *cute*. Cute? Some voyeuristic old *lech* comes in here night after night to get drunk off her ass and laugh like a hyena and stare at some eighteen-year-old messenger-boy's ass? I thought she was disgusting."

"What is this?" Sally was pointing to a small framed print nailed over the low doorjamb that led into the bar.

It was maybe eight inches by five inches, framed in antique serrated wood, cut into Aztec-looking stars. Inside the frame was a colored print of the mysterious armadillo they had seen earlier in the library.

"Some kind of ancient virility symbol, I think," said Tom. "You know who loved it? Steve. He said it was 'pyramid power' and that if you put it over the door like that it gave magical stamina to anyone who passed under it." Tom chuckled. "In his case it might have actually worked."

"Where did you get this print?" said Q.

"I think we picked it up in that weird little place on Bleeker—Exotica Erotica—the glass is all black with red lettering—it's tiny, hard to find. But it's got stuff you *never* see anywhere else."

CHAPTER EIGHTEEN

A SEANCE FOR HOUDINI

Exotica Erotica was, indeed, hard to find. Three different people on the street gave three wildly different sets of directions. It turned out to be situated between a store that sold vintage pinball machines and MacDougal Marty's Used Records. The exterior consisted of a narrow recessed doorway and one recessed window—all painted black except for a shoe-box-sized diorama visible in the middle of the glass. It displayed two white vibrators—their rounded sides pointed up in the air. One was slightly smaller than the other. Behind them was a tiny American flag on a toothpick, and beneath them a printed caption: *We Will Never Forget.*

The red lettering on the black window read: Exotica Erotica—Costumes, Masks, Magic, Object d' Art.

What sounded like sleighbells rattled as they entered the tiny store. Monster masks peered down at them: Mohawked Madman, Werewolf, Frankenstein, George W. Bush. The room smelled of strong coffee. Glass cases were filled with magical apparatus. Q. recognized some of them from his youth: Strat-O-Spheres, guillotine, nickles-to-dimes.

"We've been expecting you," said a deep-voiced man entering from behind the curtained backroom. He was an enormously overweight black man wearing a fez and a heavy-cloth white shirt. Black suspenders held up his gigantic black trousers.

"Did Tom call?" asked Sally.

"No, my dear. Your delightful appearance was announced by the tarot." He pronounced "tarot" as if it were "da-chrow." He pointed to three cards, one of them upside down, on the counter.

"And what do the cards reveal?" said Q.

"Visitors and new information! But allow me to introduce myself. I am Nicholas Nebuchadnezzar."

"That sign," said Sally, and she was pointing to his fez. "We're trying to find out what it means."

Pictured on the fez was the armadillo.

"An ancient symbol, I believe, from the fringes of Zoroastrianism. A mystical raccoon"

"We've been seeing it everywhere we go."

"And, where, my charming young woman, have you been?"

Sally looked at Q. She'd probably said too much already.

Q. said, "We saw it in an old book and—"

"By Gad, sir!" said Nebuchadnezzar loudly. "I am not a man to be trifled with. Do you have the raccoon or not?"

Sally was about to speak when Q. kicked her ankle.

"And if we had it?" said Q. "And I'm not saying that we do. But if we did? What would it be worth to you?"

"By Gad, sir! You drive a hard bargain. But let me say this, in all honesty. I am prepared to offer you one hundred thousand dollars cash, immediately, for the return of the raccoon."

"One hundred thousand dollars cash?"

"I was told you were a difficult customer, and, by Gad, sir, I can see they were right. But let me say that only makes me respect you more, sir, because, by Gad, I am a difficult customer myself. Two hundred thousand dollars for the raccoon. That is my final offer."

"The dingus is worth twice that," said Q.

"Perhaps, sir, but the risk. You are forgetting the risk. Very well, then. Two hundred and fifty thousand for, as you so charmingly refer to it, the dingus. By Gad, sir, have we a deal or not?" Nebuchadnezzar extended his large hand.

"I'll have to speak to my colleagues first," said Q. "But between you and me, Mr. Nebuchadnezzar, I think they'll go for it. In fact, I think they'll be glad to get rid of it."

"Understandable, sir. The raccoon is a dangerous artifact to have in one's possession. You are familiar with its story, of course."

"Only bits and pieces."

"Well, by Gad, sir, take a seat with your beautiful companion. And I shall join you."

He forced himself from behind the counter—got himself briefly wedged in the slot—and then yanked himself through, tearing the side of his pants.

"By Gad, sir, I have to get a smaller counter," he said. "Or stronger trousers. But, please, let me share with you some of my Turkish coffee. It is my one indulgence."

He settled himself into an armchair—while Q. and Sally sat in wooden upright chairs around a small table. Nebuchadnezzar poured them all coffees in black, thimble-sized cups. Also on the table was a tarot deck and an omnibus edition of the novels of Dashiell Hammett.

"You're a fan of Hammett?" asked Sally.

"I was named after a character in one of his stories," said Nebuchadnezzar. "*The Thin Man*. Though, I'll admit, the parallel in body type seems somewhat elusive. But drink up, sir and madam, and allow me to tell you a story the likes of which I dare say, you will never hear again—for, quite candidly, sir, I'm a man who enjoys talking to a man who likes talking to a man who likes talking to a man who likes to talk."

"...and that, my friends," said Nicholas Nebuchadnezzar as the smoke from his exotic cigarette finally dissipated in the air, "is the tale as best as I, a most humble scholar in its arcane history, can reconstruct it. And, by Gad, sir, you see now the *power*, the majesty, and the—"

"Wait a minute," said Q. who had barely taken a half-sip of his coffee. "You didn't tell us the story. You just skipped a few lines in the manuscript and started with an ellipse."

"By Gad, sir, you *are* a difficult customer. Both observant and devastatingly accurate. Sir, I admire you to no end. And, I warn you, you're being admired by a man who likes admiring a man who enjoys admiring a man who—"

"Just tell us the story? Please?"

"I shall be honored, sir, but be prepared to have the

very foundations of your beliefs in the nature of the so-called material world shaken to their core." He took a sip of his pungent coffee. "You are, as a man of the world, and your associate, as a young woman of the world, familiar with the case of the spiritualist Alicia, whose work so captured the imagination of the thrill-seeking public in the early 1920's? A modest, well-respected woman of Boston, Massachusetts; her husband, the eminent Dr. Alfred Goddard Crandon, an instructor of surgery at Harvard Medical School for sixteen years—a couple beyond fakery and charlatanism of any kind."

And here, quite extraordinarily, Mr. Nebuchadnezzar let loose an enormous fart: long, extended, modulated like a fantastic tuba howl from Stinkland. He wiped his brow with a red silk handkerchief. "Excuse me, sir. The Turkish coffee. By Gad, I practically live on it, but my large intestine, and all parts of me seem to be large, feels it must make these infernal and, regrettably, somewhat odoriferous objections. But let me return to my narrative..."

Sally looked at Q. and wrinkled her nose at the fetid emanations rising around her.

"Now, sir," continued Nebuchadnezzar. "Dr. Crandon was keenly interested in Spiritualism, having attended a lecture in 1923 by Sir Oliver Lodge, in which Lodge discussed how the medium Gladys Osborne Leonard was able to conjure the spirit of his son Raymond who had died in the Great War. Raymond had not only appeared in the room with Sir Oliver, but had asked his father if he could borrow some money.

"So fascinated were the Crandons with these stories of communication with the other world, that in May of 1923 they decided to hold a séance in an empty room at the top of their old four-story house. Joined by two friends, including Alicia's dentist, the skeptical Dr. Kasha Knisch, the sitters held hands as all the lights were extinguished. You can well imagine the scene. The room tense with expectations. Well, by Gad, sir, they did not have to wait long for psychic manifestations to appear. First, the table tilted, spilling a pitcher of water in the lap of Dr. Knisch. Then raps were heard on the table. Bells chimed somewhere in the room—though all the doors had been locked. When the lights were turned back on, it was also discovered that Dr. Knisch's yarmulke was missing.

"At any rate, in December of 1922, *Scientific American* had sponsored a contest to either prove or disprove the existence of psychic phenomenon. The magazine offered twenty-five hundred dollars to anyone who could produce visible psychic manifestations. John Malcolm Bird chaired the committee whose members included Professor William McDougall, who had recently been president of the Society for Psychical Research, Dr. Daniel Frost Comstock, Dr. Walter Franklin Stone, Heywood Carrington, the intrepid Dr. Kasha Knisch, and most notably, the famous conjurer Harry Houdini.

"Most mediums refused to accept the scientific rigor of the test conditions under which the manifestations were to be produced. Those who did accept the conditions were unable to reproduce any clearly visible phenomenon.

"By Gad, sir, that seemed to be the end of things—but then the novelist Sir Arthur Conan Doyle put forward the name of Mrs. Crandon. Doyle had attended a séance with Mrs. Crandon the previous summer in which the medium's spirit guide, her deceased brother, had spoken to Doyle and told him, first, that President Warren G. Harding would die in office and, second, that Doyle had lost a pair of eyeglasses and could find them behind the couch. Two days later Harding died returning from a trip to Alaska. However, Doyle never did find his eyeglasses, though he searched repeatedly behind the couch, and he was forced to purchase a new pair."

Nebuchadnezzar leaned in more intimately and took a sip of coffee. "It was at this time that the most curious and provocative part of the tale takes shape. One afternoon, shortly after the séance, Mrs. Crandon and Doyle were walking down the streets of Boston. Doyle, in his journals, describes a curious little table filled with a fantastic array of—"

And here, once again, the table shook as Nebuchadnezzar let loose another blast from the furnace in his pants. This time it was a high, whining one, as if he were trying desperately to contain its explosive energy. It whimpered. It sirened. It wailed like an artillery shell.

He wiped his brow. "The tale is, no doubt, sir, exciting my already highly-strained digestive system."

"Would you like some chewable papaya enzyme?" said Q., offering a roll from his breast pocket.

"By Gad, sir. This may be exactly what I've been

searching for."

"Take two."

Nebuchadnezzar shoved two orange tablets into the mountain of his face and continued.

"This table of antiquities contained what appeared to be, for all intents and purposes—how shall I call it?—a *figurine*. A decorative carved animal—fashioned entirely of wood—say, so big." He held his hands about a foot apart. "On a wooden base. It appeared to be nothing. A trinket found among other native carvings on the table. One figure was a drummer. One was a boy holding a lamb. The merchant who owned them told Doyle they were native carvings from Gozo, one of the islands of the Republic of Malta in the Sea of Sicily. But this particular figure, and the one that seemed to fascinate Alicia, was that of a perfectly carved raccoon."

"The Maltese raccoon!" said Sally.

"Exactly," said Nebuchadnezzar. He removed his fez and indicated its ornament. "A crude representation to be sure, but, still—undeniably—the figure... The merchant told Doyle the figure had come from the personal collection of Auguste Rodin, who had died seven years earlier. But, of course, no one gave the claim any credence."

"Have you ever seen the actual figure?" said Sally.

"I've held it in my hands," said Nebuchadnezzar. "Held it in these very hands. And, by Gad, if only I'd known... I'd have never let go of it." A short rasping honk emitted from his colon. "Pardon. At any rate—" Another honk. This seemed to relax his features. "I think the papaya is slowly taking effect. Ah. Well, sir, the medium Alicia insisted that Doyle buy the figurine for her. 'It is expensive,' Doyle protested, 'and you still haven't located my eyeglasses.' She insisted. 'Why?' he asked her. She answered: 'The figure has emanations. It has *power*.'

"That evening a séance was held on the fourth floor of the Crandon house, and in the center of the table was placed the figurine. The air was charged with portents. Doyle wrote that he felt electricity at the top of his head, but no obvious manifestations were produced.

"Doyle was disappointed, and he returned to his hotel room at about eleven o'clock. He was writing a letter to his wife Jean when he suddenly felt the *presence* of something extraordinary. The same electric tingling at the top of his head. He felt it might have been the presence of his son who died from wounds inflicted in the Great War. He called out his son's name: Kingsley! But there was no rapping, no levitation, no traditional manifestations of the supernormal. Instead, and by Gad, may I speak frankly, sir? I mean, with a lady present?"

Q. nodded. "Sally is the very soul of discretion, before whom you may speak as frankly as before myself."

"Well said, sir." Nebuchadnezzar removed two jade worry-balls from his pocket and nervously clicked them through his narrative. "Doyle suddenly found himself in the throes of—how shall I put this?—a wild priapic firestorm. A sense of sexual arousal overcame him that he could only describe as 'maddening.' And remember, sir, that by this time Doyle was a man in his mid-sixties—but, suddenly, on a hot Boston night, three thousand miles from his wife, he finds himself aroused with the strength and power of a man in his twenties!

"Unable to contain the seething vibrations that so violently seized his loins, he goes walking alone through the streets of Boston. It was now well past midnight, and he soon found himself in the vilest and most disreputable part of the city where the poorer women sold themselves to simply survive.

"Doyle, feeling the mad beast coursing through his veins, found solace in a poor young slattern of the streets. They rented a room in the back of a vile opium den maintained by a hideously disfigured lascar, and all through the night, again and again, Doyle pounded the poor creature. Still, he could not dissipate his fiend-like carnal desires.

"Being a doctor he naturally worried about the poor girl's health, fearing he might do damage to her young body. At one point, seeing she was anemic and malnourished, he summoned the lascar to fetch an enormous dinner. He and the girl dined on wine and fruit and vast joints of steaming beef. He reassured the young girl that he would take care of her and provide the means that she might free herself from the servitude of the streets. But, by this time, his own steaming beef had announced itself once again to the point that Doyle felt it must be answered or his seminal vesicles might spontaneously explode. And for six more hours he pleasured the woman. At two or three instances the woman fell sound asleep, but it made no difference to Doyle. He wrote that the very devil himself had overtaken his body and what he was spewing forth was foul and polluted.

"At dawn, Doyle dragged himself back to the hotel. And he awoke that afternoon—just another tired Britisher in a foreign hotel. All desire was gone. He was convinced it must have been an hallucination induced by the strain of the séances.

"He dined that night with the Crandons. At one point, when they were alone in a hallway, Mrs. Crandon whispered to him: 'Did you feel it last night?'

"'What?' he answered.

"'The *emanations*,' she said.

"What follows now is a little cloudy, but we know that apparently Alicia felt the power of the figurine as well. The next night Dr. Alfred discovered his wife and Conan Doyle in the alleyway behind their house. Doyle's trousers were down around his ankles, and Mrs. Crandon was heard exclaiming, 'It looks like a gigantic hound!'

"Doyle left the city the next day. But he recommended to the *Scientific American* contest committee that Mrs. Crandon be tested under rigidly-controlled conditions.

"The first séance took place on April 12, 1924. A Saturday.

"Alicia sat at a table illuminated with only a dim red light. Her hands were held by Dr. Crandon on the right, and by Dr. Knisch on the left. Present, also, were Dr. Walter Franklin Stone, and Professor William MacDougal. Alicia wore only a white satin robe, silk-stockings, and slippers.

"And on the table before them stood the object which Alicia now claimed helped her focus her vibrations, the carved wooden raccoon!

"Well, sir, almost immediately manifestations made themselves known: a chair overturned, the pendulum clock ceased its movement, an ectoplasmic illumination was seen hovering around Alicia's head, and all the gentlemen in the room reported the presence of what they could only describe vaguely as an energy field or energy presence. The only exception was Dr. Knisch who complained that all he felt was 'a little nauseous.'

"Houdini and his entourage arrived from New York the next day, *outraged* that he had not been present for the initial sitting. 'There's no effect that woman can produce that I can't accomplish through sleight of hand!' claimed a livid Houdini to the committee.

"'I doubt that,' said MacDougall.

"Houdini demanded to know what had been so remarkable.

"'All the committee members in the room felt a great wave of energy,' said Dr. Stone.

"'What does *that* mean?' said Houdini. 'How can you prove there was energy?'

"'It was a sort of animal-voltage,' said MacDougall.

"'What the hell are you stuffed-shirts talking about, *animal voltage?*'

"'A primal priapic urge,' said Stone. 'We felt younger. We felt in touch with something eternal and timeless and—'

"'—in other words,' said Dr. Knisch, 'they all got boners.'

"'Boners!' exclaimed Houdini. 'You're sitting here telling me the séance gave you a boner?'

"'In a manner of speaking... yes,' said Stone.

"'All *I* felt,' said Knisch, 'was a little nauseous.'

"'You people are crazy!' exclaimed Houdini. 'How can you print *that* in the *Journal for the Society of Psychical Research*? All four of the committee members reported getting erections?'

"'It may be a genuine manifestation of the supernormal,' said MacDougall.

"'Yeah, and maybe if your wife played with your ding-dong a little more—'

"'Please, please,' said Stone. 'Let's do another séance with Mr. Houdini present. Let's see what happens.'

"'Let me at her!' said Houdini. 'I can smell a fake in a kimono a mile off!'

"And so Houdini had sent from New York his 'rat trap'—his own term for the equipment he used to catch false mediums: a wooden cabinet in which only Alicia's head, hands, and ankles could protrude.

"All four members of the committee were present in the room plus Dr. Crandon.

"The 'focus object' was placed on the séance table. 'What the hell is this?' said Houdini. He examined the raccoon for false compartments or hidden magnets but found nothing.

"The lights were dimmed.

"Then the red light flickered out entirely.

"Nothing. Just the ticking of the clock in the room. Darkness... And then breaking through the silence came a powerful—"

A mighty fart erupted from Nicholas Nebuchadnezzar. He shifted his weight.

"Pardon. And from within the cabinet came a scratching noise against the wood, as if some animal were trying to escape from within. And, mind you, both Alicia's hands were being held at the time.

"Then the séance table began to tilt and vibrate and finally it actually appeared to *levitate*.

"Suddenly the lights were thrown on, and the table fell back to the ground. 'Just as I suspected!' cried out Houdini, standing by the light switch.

"'What?' asked MacDougall.

"'Uh...' said the great conjurer, looking around wildly for wires or collapsible poles or confederates of any sort.

"He was instantly on his knees crawling around under the table. 'Yes, exactly!' he proclaimed.

"Then he examined the locks on the cabinet and the armholes and the neckhole. 'I've seen it all before,' said Houdini. 'Eusapia Palladini, Franck Kluski, Willi and Rudi Schneider—all very convincing to the untrained eye.'

"'But the table?' said Dr. Stone. 'The vibrations? The levitation?'

"'Easily accomplished with powerful magnets hidden within the hollowed-out table legs and carefully placed on corresponding electro-magnetic plates within the floor.

The plates are charged; polarized with the opposite charge of the corresponding table legs—'

"'Mr. Houdini,' pleaded Dr. Crandon. 'This is an ordinary table. Examine it. There are no electromagnetic plates under the floor.'

"'None that I can *see*,' said the magician. 'But if I take this quarter and place it in my palm and close my fist around it thusly.' He had placed a twenty-five cent piece into his small hand. 'And if I open my hand and the coin has mysteriously vanished!' Indeed the coin *had* vanished. 'Does that mean the coin has dematerialized into the spirit realm? I ask the good doctor. Where is the coin?'

"'It's in your other hand,' said Crandon. 'I can see it through your fingers.'

"'Yes, well, perhaps,' said Houdini, quickly placing his hand into his pocket.

"Houdini immediately wanted to repeat the séance, but Dr. Knisch complained that he had a little headache. 'It's nothing terrible,' he said. 'But I should take an aspirin before it gets worse.'

"That night, sir, the same phenomenon that had so affected Conan Doyle played itself out on Dr. Kasha Knisch. Unable to sleep, he told his wife, shortly after midnight, that he was preoccupied with a difficult dental problem, and needed to walk.

"He apparently took a cab to an upscale house of ill-repute frequented by the best of Boston society, and there he moved from room to room until he had spent himself in the company of a dozen different women. He walked downstairs, drank a glass of wine, chanted the *Shema*, and then proceeded to visit the same twelve women again, this time in backwards order.

"He arrived home seven hours later.

"'And where have you been?' his wife asked.

"'I was out filling cavities,' he replied.

"'They must have been awfully big.'

"'Darling, you couldn't imagine.'

"The next night at the séance Houdini arrived with boards, nails, and a hammer. This time he proceeded to nail Mrs. Crandon inside the cabinet. He boarded up the armholes, the footholes, and the neckhole. He nailed bracing boards to the sides and bottom. He then insisted that if Dr. Crandon were to remain in the room, he must be handcuffed and roped to his chair. After some protestation, the doctor agreed to these conditions, and the poor man was manacled and tethered to a rocking chair while his poor wife was imprisoned in the wooden box.

"'Now we shall see about psychic manifestations!' cried Houdini in a sweat of excitement.

"The lights were dimmed...

"There was a long, ominous silence...

"The men could hear each other breathing.

"Even the clock had been stopped so that the scientists might not miss the slightest noise.

"And then, from the darkness—

A wild grand-finale of a fart, the sound a man might produce after being constipated for thirty years, belched and squealed and splattered and quaked and pulsed and howled its horrible, suffocating, malodorous release into the air of the tiny shop.

"Oh, my God," said Sally. "I can't breathe."

"Pardon, pardon," said Nebuchadnezzar. "But you must listen because this is the part of the tale that most concerns you."

"She's locked in the cabinet," said Q.

"Yes," said Nebuchadnezzar. "But the figurine, the raccoon, is still sitting on the séance table. And in the total darkness of the room the figurine can be seen outlined in a faintly luminous glow. Then a pair of hands, *real* hands, grabs the figurine, cloaks it in darkness for a half-second. And then there are footsteps running towards the door! The door is thrown open—and footsteps are heard tearing down the stairs.

"Houdini switches on the lights.

"The dentist, Doctor Knisch, is gone! And so is the raccoon.

"All three scientists go hurtling down the stairs to find him—leaving poor Doctor Crandon still tied and handcuffed to his rocking chair and his dear wife boarded up in a wooden cabinet.

"The scientists have reached the street in front of the four-story home, but there is no sign of the dentist."

Nebuchadnezzar got up from his chair.

"Dr. Kasha Knisch was never seen again."

CHAPTER NINETEEN

THE DINGUS

"And the raccoon?" said Q.

"Ah! The raccoon... For nearly eighty years men have been pursuing it. Its origins seem, indeed, to be from the island of Gozo. It is consistent with certain other native carvings from the mid-16th century. We know on the Maltese Islands the existence of an obscure cult called, variously, the Royal Order of Raccoons or the International Order of Friendly Raccoons. The cult apparently still exists—a kind of secret society whose leader is known as the Grand High Exalted Mystic Raccoon."

"Wait a minute, this sounds like *The Honeymooners*," said Sally. "You know, where Ralph is trying to get elected Raccoon of the Year."

"By Gad, how singularly observant you are!" said Nebuchadnezzar. "You will recall one of the men at the original séance was Dr. Walter Franklin Stone. His son, also Walter Stone, was the television writer who, in the 1950's, with his partner Marvin Marx, wrote most of *The Honeymooners* episodes. Stone clearly knew of the figurine, of its rich, fantastical history, and deliberately made references to the material within the fabric of the show. As you say, the Raccoon Lodge. Mrs. Alicia Crandon becomes 'Alice Kramden.' Dr. Alfred Crandon becomes 'Ralph.' It's a subtle and pervasive subtext and surely intended as a deliberate sign, to members of the secret society all over the world, and now through *time*, that the figure still exists among us—still exerts its strange and provocative powers.

"And the figure, indeed, seems to have once belonged to the artist August Rodin—which explains, perhaps, what the great 'Thinker' has been contemplating all these many years: Why he can no longer achieve an erection. Haha! You'll pardon my attempt at a wry witticism. But the raccoon's history is littered with deception. How it came to appear on the table of Boston flea market in 1924 we may never know. Some people consider the figure demonic. Others feel it is the embodiment of the *animus*—the vital male spirit. But *none*, sir, can deny its power."

He reached behind the counter to the Halloween masks and removed a Davy Crockett-style coonskin cap. "I hope you will accept this," he said to Sally, "as a gift from an admirer of both your rare beauty and your even rarer powers of perception!"

She smiled and put it on. Then she waved the pelt and warbled the Raccoon salute: "wooooooo!"

"Excellent" said Nebuchadnezzar. "You are truly one of the chosen. And now, sir, you've heard my offer: two hundred and fifty thousand dollars for the figurine. I take it that is acceptable?"

"You feel it's worth all that?" said Q.

"By Gad, sir, I consider that cheap." He whispered:

"Think, sir, what that *power* would be worth? Think how men would hunger for it. To feel again the mad panther of youth! To submerge oneself again into the torrent of pure carnality. And, sir, I'm told it has the same effect on women. Some say for women it is even more potent! It is, sir, to risk hyperbole, a modern day fountain of youth! Disciples and supplicants will flock to these portals from all over the earth. This humble store will be its temple! And its God, the Maltese Raccoon!"

"Fountain of youth?" said Sally on the train home. "Fountain of jiz is more like it. I gotta tell you, Q., maybe it's 'cause I'm a girl, but this whole thing creeps me out a little."

"It certainly is strange."

"A bunch of sick fortune-hunters running around after the Golden Phallus—getting tattooed with raccoons, holding séances, looking for cryptic messages in *The Honeymooners*? Can we say the word 'insane'?"

"You do look cute in the cap."

"Don't get any ideas." She waved the pelt. "Wooooooo!"

There was a shouting at the other end of the PATH car. Someone had shoved a door open between the moving cars and was pushing people out of the way.

Sally saw him first, and, literally, her jaw dropped.

It was Steve, the darling of The Bulgin' Marbles, the Studhorse of Sheridan Square, who had been bar-hopping with Lilian Jackson Braun the night she was killed.

It was her boyfriend.

Sally stood up. "Oh, my God."

Her first thought was that he had come to kill her—right here on the PATH train—and in those first crazy seconds she already saw her death on the floor of the train, staring up at the bottom of a plastic seat, the floorboards roaring in her ears.

Now Q. was standing.

Steve was incoherent as he approached—pale, his eyes unfocused, his mouth bubbling, not walking but staggering forward in his sneakers. He wore Hawaiian shorts and a sleeveless tee-shirt—on his right shoulder was the raccoon tattoo—and in his hands was a wrapped package. It was about the size of a shoebox—irregular in shape, wrapped in brown paper and brown waterproof mailing tape.

His face and hands were scratched as if he'd run through thorns.

The passengers were standing in horror now. A woman screamed.

Steve thumped messily before Sally and held out the package to her. He was blinking his eyes rapidly, trying to stay focused. The expression on his face was somewhere between exhaustion and pleading and love.

He pushed the package into her hands.

"Baby, you're the greatest," he said, then fell forward onto the floor.

Sally cried out.

Sticking out from his back was the shaft of an arrow.

"Steve," said Sally, and she touched his back with something like an explosion of grief rising up from her heart—

—but now there was a noise from the *other* end of the car. Through the closed door of their car, Sally could see in the next car a pack of overweight men shoving and swearing as they ran towards the near-door.

The men were dressed in what appeared to be movie usher uniforms with gold braid on the shoulders and Davy Crockett-style coonskin caps.

And they were running towards Sally and Q.

"Grab the dingus!" said Q.

He took her hand and pulled hard.

CHAPTER TWENTY

BANG, ZOOM

"Wooooooo!"

The warbling of the Raccoons followed close on their heels as they ran through the PATH cars.

The chief Raccoon, who looked remarkably like Jackie Gleason with a Mohawk, led the pack with a crossbow slung over his shoulder.

Q. ran forward, wondering whether the chief Raccoon would have enough nerve to fire the weapon in a crowded train car.

Thwak!

A hunting arrow had penetrated an advertisement eight inches away from his head. The ad was for Target stores, and the arrow had scored a bull's-eye.

Sally, who was faster than he was, now led the way.

Ahead of her, completely blocking the aisle, stood a woman behind a double-baby stroller. The woman was on a cell phone, talking at the top of her voice over the train noise. "He said that the cysts are normal, and that I should expect bleeding."

"If you don't get out of the way, you can expect more bleeding," said Sally, scrambling to get past her.

Q. also tried to squeeze by, and in the process lost his right shoe which he did not go back to retrieve.

"Hey!" a passenger shouted. "Here!"

Q. turned to see a male passenger hurling a shoe towards him.

The shoe missed him by ten feet and smashed into a little bald man who was reading *The Wall Street Journal*. He fell right over.

As they pushed through the next set of sliding doors, Q. looked back to see the overweight Raccoons struggling to get past the woman with the double-stroller. They were piling up behind each other—hopelessly log-jammed.

The train was pulling into Newark station now, and as Q. and Sally exited from the PATH car, the Raccoons also streamed out through the crowded platform.

There were both stairs and an escalator descending from the platform, and Sally took the steps at a run.

"Come on!" she yelled, and this time *she* was pulling hard.

Q. was winded. "You're a professional runner," he said. "I'm just a middle-aged guy with one shoe."

"Come on, you old fart!"

"Wooooooo!" the Raccoons were howling behind them.

Sally looked around at the various directions to run.

"We got to find a cop!"

"And what are you going to tell him?" asked Q. "That we're being chased by Raccoons?"

"Come on! I've got a plan."

She pulled him in tow down towards the PATH stairs

for the New York-bound line. Under her arm she still clutched the package Steve had given her.

"We're getting *back* on the train?"

"If we can outrun 'em," said Sally.

They were running *up* a staircase now.

Thwak!

A tomahawk spun directly into the advertisement next to her shoulder. It was a poster for singer Ed Ames' Greatest Hits—and the tomahawk pierced Ames right in the crotch.

The chief Raccoon was reloading his crossbow as Sally and Q. moved out of his sightline.

The New York City-bound PATH train was just emptying its passengers as Sally pushed her way towards the turnstile.

She effortlessly vaulted over it—gesturing to Q. to follow.

He tried once: a desperate, weighty man in a white sports jacket and a Panama hat. He wasn't even close.

He opened his wallet; there were only two twenties inside—and the machine would only take a dollar and a half.

The change machine was glowing green: Temporarily Unavailable.

The Quick-Pass machine: Needs Service.

"Can I borrow a buck and half?" he asked a stranger.

He was ignored.

"Hey, I'll give you twenty dollars for a buck and a half."

"Fuck you."

"Come on!" yelled Sally.

Q. was spinning around helplessly.

"Go under it!"

And so, on his knees, he crawled over the filthy floor, and under the turnstile.

People were stuffing their passes into the turnstiles around him.

"Hey, man, what the hell are you doing?"

"Look, mommy, that man is crawling on the floor."

"That's exactly the kind of man mommy told you *never* to talk to."

Sally pulled him up.

"I'm getting too old for this," said Q.

Somebody screamed—and Q. turned to hear *thwak!* about two feet away. The arrow had penetrated a soda machine featuring a bikini-clad blonde holding a Pepsi. It pierced the center of her forehead and Pepsi spurted straight out of her breasts as cans of soda started dropping out of the machine.

Sally pulled him onboard the train. They ran down the length of one car—and hid out of sight *between* the cars.

From their vantage point they could see the Raccoons struggling with the turnstiles. They also had no singles—plus their girths held them pinned between the metal arms.

Now one was through.

It was the Chief.

But the doors were closing.

The train was pulling out of Newark station.

Wooooooo!

A Raccoon on the platform had spotted them. He was alerting someone on his cell phone.

"They'll be waiting for us at Jersey City," said Sally.

"Maybe we should just ditch the dingus." Q. was looking at the parcel.

"Are you kidding? I wanna see if this thing works on women like he said."

"Don't look now, but here comes Raccoon of the Year."

One of the Lodge Brothers was two cars away, cellphone in hand, heading in their direction.

"The cars are numbered," said Sally. "He's telling his friends. We've got to get out of this one."

She moved towards the next car.

"Sally, it's a train; there's nowhere to hide."

"Did you ever try?"

They pushed their way through the standing passengers.

"May I make a suggestion?" said Q.

"What?"

"Lose the hat. You're too easy to spot."

"Hey, you lose the hat. I like mine."

"I have a *reason* to wear mine," said Q., jostling into a large woman drinking a bottle of Fiji water.

The water bottle spilled all over her dress and fell to the floor.

"Damn," she said.

"Sorry."

"Why the fuck are you people in such a hurry?"

"Because people are trying to kill us," said Q., pushing past her.

"I can see why. You come back this way and *I'll* try to kill you."

"So what's your reason for the hat?" asked Sally.

"I'm trying to cover the bald spot, OK? I'm trying to look young and vital, when I'm old and embittered. This way if they kill me, they can at least say, 'God, he looked so young.'"

"That's important."

"And *you* look like Davy Crockett's understudy in the Middle School play."

"Stop that man!" called a voice down the car.

It was the Raccoon standing in the middle of the car pointing at Q.

"Stop him, please! He's kidnapped my daughter! For God's sake, *somebody stop him!*"

One hundred and ten pairs of outraged eyes turned towards Q.

"Look. I didn't kidnap *any*body," said Q. He held up his hands as they continued to run through the car. "Nobody's kidnapping anybody, see? I'm not touching her. OK?"

"I'm fine!" yelled Sally. "I'm perfectly fine! But that man—" and she stopped to point back at the Raccoon "—tried to rape me! Somebody stop him! Somebody stop him and call 9-1-1."

One hundred and ten cell phones were instantly activated.

"You tried to *rape* that little girl!" roared the woman

with the Fiji water stains. "Damn, I'll kill you myself!"

The Raccoon tried to get out of her path, but he slipped on the water—went down on the floor—and she began to beat him with her shoulder bag. "You run, girl!" she called to Sally. "We got this covered!"

"Thank you!"

Sally pulled the sliding glass door closed behind her. "Look," she said. "They're going to be waiting for us in Jersey City. There's no way we're going to get past a whole station of them. We gotta get off here."

"The train doesn't stop here."

They were crossing through what looked like an industrial switching station.

"Now it does," said Sally, and she pulled the emergency stop cord.

It did absolutely nothing.

She pulled again.

"Look at this! It's a joke. It doesn't even do anything."

"It's the special New Jersey emergency cord."

From her knapsack she pulled out the Newberry-Award-Losing letter opener.

She jiggled around the blade in the door of the control closet that said: No Unauthorized Entry.

"What are you doing?"

"Maybe I can stop the—"

The door opened part way—like the hood of a car—and Sally got her small fingers in the crack and manipulated the latch.

She turned the rotary handle and the door opened.

To both their astonishment it was not a control closet at all, but a tiny bathroom—obviously designed to accommodate only the train personnel. It was about the size of a toilet on an airplane.

"Look at this!" said Sally.

"You can only take a piss on this train if you're a member of the Teamsters."

"Jersey City, next stop. Jersey City Station," garbled the overhead voice.

"Get in," said Sally.

"Yeah."

"I'm serious. We've got to hide. It's the only way."

"We can't both fit in there."

"We're gonna have to. Come on, lard-ass, inside."

The effect was like one of those old fraternity stunts about jamming ten people into a phone booth.

The ceiling was too low to allow standing on the toilet—so they ended up cradled like spoons, Sally in front of him, as she jammed the door shut and turned the rotary lock.

"Now just shut up and pray to God nobody on this train has to take a leak," she said.

Q. had his arms around her, and what he was actually praying for was that he wouldn't get a hard-on.

"We'll stay hidden till we get to New York," whispered Sally. "Then we can get lost in the crowd. They're never going to find us there."

"Absolutely."

He tried to think about funerals.

Death. Tombstones. Grieving widows. Hearses.

"What's that in your pocket?" she asked.

Coffins. Shovels.

"It's the letter opener."

"I've got the letter opener. Oh, *Jesus*, Q."

"I'm trying. I'm sorry, Sally. I'm really trying."

"Oh, Jesus. Please, God. I thought you and I had an understanding."

"We *do* have an understanding. Believe me."

"*I* believe you," said Sally. "I just don't think your little friend is so convinced."

"It's not my fault. Really. It has a life of its—I'm thinking good thoughts; I really am."

Rotting corpses. Skeletons.

"Stop moving it around."

"I'm not moving it."

"Well, who's moving it then?"

"I told you; it has its own mind."

"Talk to it."

"I can't. I don't speak Testicle."

"You know, Steve was always telling me, 'How can you work for him? He's such a dirty old man.' And I said, 'He's not a dirty old man, he's a sweet, middle-aged guy.'"

"I *am* a sweet middle-aged guy."

"Then get that tire-iron out of my ass!"

"It's not my fault—I think it's the figurine."

"What?"

"You now, the raccoon. I think it has magical powers. I swear it does."

"Oh, that's the *lamest* excuse I ever heard in my life."

"It's true! I swear to you. I never have feelings like this for you."

"Quiet. I hear people outside."

They must have been at one of the lower Manhattan stops, as there was a great deal of noise and transit outside the door.

They stayed still until the train began moving again.

"It's getting worse," said Sally.

"I give up," said Q.

"If you jiz on my back, I'm calling a cop."

"I'm not going to jiz on your back. It's the fucking raccoon, I told you."

"If it's the fucking raccoon, then how come I don't feel anything? Isn't it supposed to be more powerful for women?"

"You're asking me! And another thing. *Steve* is calling *me* a dirty old man? The guy shtupped every orifice in lower Manhattan and Northern New Jersey. And he's calling *me* a dirty old man?"

"He just didn't understand our relationship."

"Well, I hope you do," said Q.

"I thought I did—until I met Mr. Crowbar."

They exited at 33rd Street—to some bewildered looks from the commuters as they fell out of the toilet together.

"It's not what you think," said Q.

"Are you all right, girl?" asked the Fiji water woman.

"I'm fine."

"You stay away from him. He nasty!"

"I'm not nasty."

Sally turned towards him. "I think you better buy some ice water, dude."

They rose up the escalator towards the cabstand. Their eyes searched the crowd—and everyone seemed to be a conspirator; *everyone* seemed to be watching. Every cell phone seemed to be a weapon against them.

They got into a cab.

The recording said: "Hi, this is Bernard Goetz; you know, people used to call me the subway shooter. But nowadays I take a cab. It's much safer. And when I take a cab, I always make sure to buckle my seatbelt."

"Just drop us off near Times Square," said Sally—and as the words left her lips she saw him across the street, in front of the Hotel Pennsylvania.

The chief Raccoon, with the mohawk, on a cell phone.

Over his shoulder was the crossbow.

They got out of the cab near that statue of the Jewish tailor in the garment district, and they walked north.

Again, every eye seemed to be on them: the faces in the coffee shops staring at them over the edge of their novels; the religious speaker with one good eye—the other a milky, unseeing gray.

Sally suddenly stopped.

"That's what he said." She was pointing ahead. "When Steve died, that's what he told me."

Two blocks down 42nd Street, at the Crazy-

Guggenheim Performing Arts Center, the marquee spirit-
edly proclaimed: BABY, YOU'RE THE GREATEST! *The
Honeymooners Musical. All dancing! All singing! All flying!*
An illuminated graphic showed a Jackie Gleason-type bus
driver with wings sprouting out of his back.

A few guys in movie usher coats and raccoon-pelt
hats were walking into the stage entrance.

Q. pulled Sally behind a newspaper kiosk.

"Those aren't the bad guys," she said. "That's the guy
from *Dirty Dancing*."

She was right. The actor Jerry Orbach was entering
the stage door, reading a copy of *Backstage*. Behind him
walked a wild-haired actor wearing a bright blue tee-shirt
which was printed with a graphic of a white life preserver; printed in black on the life preserver was Raccoon
Island—and peering out from the center was a malevo-
lent-looking raccoon face.

"We've got to get in there," Sally said. "Steve was giving me some kind of clue."

"How do you know he just wasn't saying he loved you.
Maybe he thought you *were* the greatest. It's not a bad
curtain line."

Sally looked at him. "Not to get too personal here, Q.,
but Steve thought I was far from the greatest."

"I'm sure you're wrong."

"No. There were certain things that—let's just say I
didn't like doing? If you get my meaning? I would. But I
didn't like to."

"If it's any consolation, *I* think you're the greatest,

Sally. You're wonderful and smart and funny."

An elderly couple was passing by.

"Isn't that *sweet*," said the woman who, apparently, had overheard them.

"You want to *eat*?" said the man, who, apparently, was somewhat hard of hearing. "We just ate five minutes ago."

"No, no, I said it was nice to see something a little sentimental before the big finale."

"What?"

"I said it was nice to *see*."

"You should have thought of that before we left the restaurant."

The first act of *Baby, You're The Greatest* was starting. As the show was still in previews, Q. and Sally had been able to scarf up some seats in the orchestra.

"And what exactly are we looking for?" said Q.

"There's something here," said Sally. "Something we're supposed to find out. I just know it."

The curtain opened to "traveling music," and the entire stage was filled with color and movement: Brooklyn citizens from the 1950's—with their baby carriages and lunch boxes and school books and attaché cases swarmed the stage. In the background stood the exterior of an apartment building, and next to it, in blinking neon, a restaurant announced itself as The Hong Kong Gardens. Alongside was Garrity's Pet Store—whose crooked, stylized sign was the image of the Maltese Raccoon.

Sally was pointing this out as the singing began.

CITIZENS CHORUS: Away we go!
                           Away we go!
                           It's Friday night in Bensonhurst,
                           And what a show.

OTHER CITIZENS: We're just plain folks.
                           We ain't the literati.
                           I'm Garrity!
                           I'm Ed!
                           I'm Mrs. Manicotti!

MRS. MANICOTTI: *(spoken)* Hey, Mr. Garrity, you hear our Ralph's gonna be on a quiz show tonight!

GARRITY: *(spoken)* Yeah, I hear he's gonna be the biggest thing on television!

Sally was pulling at Q.'s arm. "Look at her dress," she said—and her eyes indicated an actress in a plain housedress. "Look at her belt."

Q. hadn't even noticed the dress had a belt, but now he saw it was a gray sash—and stitched in lavender on the sash was the image of the Maltese Raccoon.

"Look at the Chinese restaurant," said Sally. "The sign in the window."

Sure enough, among the Mandarin characters in the window of The Hong Kong Gardens was the Maltese Raccoon.

And then Q. began to see it. It was in the scrollwork of

the streetlamps in the city set. It was in a shadow cast on the back brick wall of the theatre. It was on the lapel pin on the cop's uniform. It was the clasp on a housewife's pocketbook. It was printed on a little leaguer's bat. "What's going on?" Q. whispered. "Do you think they're all in on it?"

"I don't know," said Sally.

> ENTIRE CHORUS: The love songs in this neighborhood
> Ain't whispered by no crooners
> Just lend an ear,
> And you can hear,
> Our favorite Honeymooners...

The CHORUS points to an upstairs window where a fat man's silhouette can be seen against the window shade.

> VOICE IN APARTMENT: *(bellowing)* One of these days, Alice! One of these days!

"Why?" said Q.

"It's some kind of cult?" said Sally.

"Hiding as a Broadway show?"

"What better place to hide? You've got an audience in your grip, in the dark, for three hours."

"To do what?"

"I don't know," said Sally. "Brainwashing? Some kind of subliminal conditioning. It's creepy. Look at it! It's all over the place!"

A child's bike rode across the stage, and the Maltese

Raccoon was stitched on the red saddlebag.

"And if the show's a hit, they put out road companies," said Q. "All over the country... All over the world."

"And CD's of the cast record. Millions of them. It's some kind of sick religion, Q. Some kind of *worship* of this thing. Every night. Six nights a week. And matinees." Sally shook her head in disbelief. "It's a religion, like Nebuchadnezzar said. A temple. Worshipping some unholy phallic symbol. These people are slaves to it... Steve was warning me."

ENTIRE CHORUS: Bang, zoom!
                          Night and day,
                          You hear him holler.
                          Bang, zoom!
MRS. MANICOTTI: Some day he gonna bust a collar!

A flashlight beam came flitting and probing along the aisle.

Then the voice of a female usher: "Hey, you can't come in here without—"

She was shoved out of the way. Some sort of commotion was happening at the rear of the theatre. Q. heard other voices:

"He's got a weapon!"

"You can't—"

"Call the police! Somebody call the—"

Now even the actors onstage sensed something was wrong—their eyes moved to the back of the house, and their "bang-zooms" fell into the air without conviction.

Q. saw him first—taller than the rest.

It was the Chief Raccoon in the Mohawk.

A dozen of his Lodge Brothers were moving down the aisles.

One of them had an electronic palm-sized device—it was blinking and beeping—some kind of location device.

Since the men were dressed as Raccoons much of the audience responded as if they were part of the show— laughing and even applauding as the men storm-trooped down the aisles.

"How could they find us in the middle of—" began Sally.

"The hat!" said Q. "The fucking hat!" He grabbed Sally's coonskin cap and whipped it, frisbee-like, towards the stage.

With a deft, one-handed catch, Jerry Orbach caught it and put it instantly on his head.

He got an enormous hand from the audience.

Orbach laughed himself, took a step downstage, and apparently improvised. "As retiring Raccoon of the Year, allow me to say a few words on behalf of my friend Ralph Kramden."

The crowd loved him.

"Harry, he's funny!" said a woman whose last speaking part had been in the screen version of *The Producers*.

By this point, Sally was climbing over the seats—and two Raccoons were closing in on her from the aisle.

"Sally!" yelled Q. He raised his hands over his head.

She instantly tossed him the parcel—he stuffed it under his sports coat, and moved in the opposite direction.

"The big one's got it!" came a voice from the far aisle. "The guy!"

"Listen, fellas!" called Orbach from the stage. He looked at his watch. "The Raccoons aren't meeting till the second act, so if you guys want to come back around nine-thirty—"

The audience roared its approval.

Now there were hands on Q's sportscoat.

And Sally was up on the backs of the theatre seats—balancing along the spines—then she jumped into the center aisle.

"They're behind you!" she cried.

Q. fumbled—and half slipped out of his sports coat, and he threw the package towards Sally.

He was way too high—but as the package descended she vaulted off an arm rest and made a flying catch.

Now the audience applauded *her*.

And she was laughing from the pure exhilaration of her effort.

She turned towards the orchestra.

They were coming up at her from the orchestra.

She moved up the aisle—but they were bearing down hard towards her from that direction as well, and leading the pack was the Mohawk Raccoon who held before him now a wicked-looking knife.

Long and curved like a machete.

"Sally!" Q. cried out.

She turned back towards the stage, and with all the strength her arms could gather, she hurled the package towards the stage like a discus.

It sailed in a perfect, spinning arc towards the actors who stood frozen on stage.

Jerry Orbach raised both his arms over his head like an Olympic athlete in victory—and he caught the package between his hands.

He smiled.

The actor next to him, playing Ed Norton, was still delivering his lines, frantically attempting to keep the show going. "I wish somebody would invent something that could do the work of *all* of these things!" He spun around and found himself facing Orbach. "And who are *you?!*"

The audience was poised to applaud, but in the split-second before it could, there was a terrible SWOOOOSH! and the long, curved machete went spinning through the air over the orchestra pit—every eye in the theatre was on it and—THWICK!—the blade buried itself deep in the center of Orbach's chest.

For a second he stood there stunned.

The entire theatre was motionless and silent.

"And who are *you?*" said the actor playing Ed Norton, still on auto-pilot.

Orbach tried to speak his lines. His mouth moved but no words came out. He looked at the other actor. At the audience. At the blade. Then he finally pulled the machete out of his chest—and held out the knife before him. His shirt was spreading with blood. He looked at the knife. *"Ch—ch—chef of the future!"* he finally said.

Then he collapsed onto the stage.

The woman playing Alice screamed.

And the curtain fell.

Chaos.

The audience started screaming and running for the doors.

There were police sirens then. The doors to the theatre flew open and what seemed like one hundred police SWAT teams were streaming down the aisles, onto the stage.

"NYPD!" yelled a voice through a megaphone. "Stay where you are!"

A man in a baseball cap holding a videocamera yelled out: "One more time, so we have it both ways, OK?"

"NYPA!" came a voice through the megaphone. "Nobody move!"

"Thank you!"

Then the officers stormed the place.

In one second, it seemed, the Chief Raccoon had been pinned and handcuffed.

The arresting officer noticed something strange about the Raccoon's face. He was wearing a full-face rubber mask.

The officer pulled it off, revealing the skin of a black man.

It was Nicholas Nebuchadnezzar.

"By Gad, sir, you've got me," muttered Nebuchadnezzar, and let loose a paint-shriveling fart.

CHAPTER TWENTY-ONE

BIZARRE CRIMES SOLVED

Detective "Perca" Dan Davies' office was, as he liked it best, filled with reporters. All of West 10th Street was clogged with soundtrucks and Eyewitness News teams.

The cops had stopped the terrorists.

Or so the public version of the story seemed to play.

A group of Davy Crockett-hat-wearing anarchists, bent on creating chaos in New York City, and believed to be loosely affiliated with al-Qaeda, were stopped dead in their tracks when cell phone calls from a car-full of PATH train riders alerted police to the anarchists' whereabouts. NYPD Emergency Interventions Teams and Manhattan F.B.I. agents traced the terrorists to a crowded theatre on 42nd Street where twenty-two of them were wrestled to the ground and arrested. One officer was injured.

The noted Broadway and Hollywood actor Jerry Orbach was also slightly injured when a knife was hurled into the flying harness he was wearing beneath his costume.

A flying Ralph Kramden?

"Well," Orbach later told reporters, "when audiences pay a hundred bucks for a ticket, they want a *show*, you know?—and in this show, *everybody* goes to the moon!"

The mysterious figurine of a raccoon was sealed in an evidence bag and sent to the F.B.I. lab in Washington, where it was found to be harmless.

It was recognized, however, as a powerful symbol of America's triumph over the axis of evil, and the image of the raccoon became the official flag of the Office of Homeland Security.

Two months later, the murderer of Lilian Jackson Braun confessed and was taken into custody in New Jersey.

Q. met with the murderer in a hospital room at New Jersey State Prison. The murderer was lying in bed watching re-runs of *Laugh-In*. An oxygen tube was clipped to his nose.

"Why the fuck not?" said Philip Roth. "She sucked as a writer." He coughed and spit up into some Kleenex.

"But killing her, Roth?"

"Hey, I'm *dying* here, OK? When *you've* got a month to live, then talk to me about your big morality."

"Bro, you didn't even know her."

"I just hate that old-school, Gentile-drek, lace-cuffed, sanitized school of writing. God, it just makes me sick."

"But still—"

"So I was sitting in that faygel bar 'cause I felt like getting my dick sucked by a guy *once* before I die; I mean, I don't have too many more to go, you know? I want to try every combination. So I see that old broad, and somebody told me who she was. And I thought, 'You know, the world doesn't need any more shitty novels,' so I followed her back to the bathroom, and I saw there was a hacksaw lying on the floor, and, what the fuck, I cut her head off. Christ, I was a little drunk and strung-out on pain-killers. So sue me, all right? So I washed my hands, went out, got my dick sucked, and drove home. OK, not the *proudest* night of my life, but, Q., I am so beyond kissing people's asses now, I don't care. My lungs are filling with shit and it can't be stopped. I'm completely *unmoored* from any kind of traditional morality. I'm beginning to have a cosmic perception. It's so fucking liberating, I can't tell you."

"You're fucking nuts, Philip."

"Maybe... But you know what I'd like right this second? You know what you can bring me? And this is a dying man's request."

"What?"

"A big-ass pastrami sandwich. So I throw half of it the fuck away! Who gives a shit?!" He indicated the television. "This show cracks me up. I can't stop watching it." Then he conducted his hands before him and sang along with the *Laugh-In* news:

What's the news across the nation?
We have got the information,
In a way, we hope will amuuuuse
Youuuuuse!

"I ought to be a singer," he said and coughed messily. He snapped his fingers like a cartoon-version of a jazz musician. "Yo, man! I'm the cat who killed Lilian Jackson Braun!" He turned back to the television. "This show is a fucking riot, man. Oh, look, here's the best part—I love the dirty old man." He coughed again.

A female social worker, dressed all in brown, came in, alarmed at his coughing.

Roth did his dirty old man voice for her: "Say? You wanna play knick-knack on my drum! Heh-heh-heh."

She beat him over the head with her handbag.

It was dawn and Sallybikerun stood in her shorts, running shoes, and *They Might Be Giants* tee-shirt next to her car. She had come to say goodbye to Q. before she headed out for her second year at Dartmouth. The car was packed with suitcases and stereo equipment—and one boyfriend. On the roof stood two bicycles.

"It's been quite a summer," she said.

"If I had known it would be so dangerous, I never would have—"

"Well, 'dangerous,' that's what you always called me. Right?"

"I suppose so."

"And I called you 'gentle'! I think I better revise that now that I've been stuck with you in a bathroom."

"Hey, I apologized for that."

They watched two squirrels chase each other along the limb of a tree—leap onto a telephone wire—and then cross to the roof of the house.

"I want to beat the traffic on the Connecticut Turnpike," she said.

"Sure."

"I'll see you Christmas, right?"

"I hope so. I mean, I'll be here. Give me a call?"

She nodded.

"Could I work again for you?" she said. "On my vacations?"

"I hope you would." There was a guy sitting on the front seat of the car. "That's Eddie, is he?"

"Yeah," said Sally a little dismissively. "He's coming for the drive. Which is nice. And then he's taking the train home."

"Another member of your fan club?"

She shrugged.

"I hope you'll put me down as a member, too," he said. "The Oldest Living Member?"

"I'll make you a plaque," said Sally. "And give you an engraved walker if you like." She looked at the ground. "Well," she said. "I'll miss you. And your cats."

"I'll miss you, too. I'll miss the sound of your bike pulling up into the driveway. The way you rang that bell."

"Emma Peel and John Steed, they don't hug, do they?" she said.

"No," he said. "I don't think so."

She extended her hand. He shook it.

It was warm.

"See you Christmas," she said.

"We've got to stop meeting like this," he said. "I think Harold is getting suspicious."

.JUN   2007

Kaplow, Robert
The cat who killed Lilian
    Jackson Braun